DAWN LEE MCKENNA & AXEL BLACKWELL

DEAD CENTER

A STILL WATERS SUSPENSE NOVEL– BOOK 2

2018

A SWEET TEA PRESS PUBLICATION

First published in the United States by Sweet Tea Press

Edited by Debbie Maxwell Allen

Cover by Shayne Rutherford
wickedgoodbookcovers.com

Interior Design by Colleen Sheehan
ampersandbookinteriors.com

ISBN: 978-0998666938

for
Matthew
my littlest boy, but my biggest fan

—Dawn Lee

&

for
The guy who cut me off on I-5 one mile before the speed
trap and ended up getting the ticket instead of me.
Thanks.
—Axel

ONE

IT WAS EARLY Saturday morning, a late-January morning that many native Floridians considered frigid and dangerous, given that the mercury had barely crept up to twenty degrees. Even worse, the gleefully melodramatic weather forecasters proclaimed that it might get down to the mid-teens that night. This wasn't unheard of that far north, but it was fairly rare. While the native Floridians bundled up and prepared to descend upon Wal-Mart to buy all the space heaters, the northern transplants shook their heads and vowed to stay off the roads.

Sergeant Ruben Goff and Deputy Jimmy Crenshaw were heading out to do welfare checks on some of Port St. Joe's older citizens, ensuring they had safe and adequate heating systems. Goff was a local, and he knew from past experience that they were going to get roped into looking at plenty of pictures of grandkids while they nibbled slightly stale oatmeal cookies.

They got the call shortly after 8:30 in the morning. Apparently, a somewhat hysterical woman had called to report a body, and something about an alligator, in the pond behind the Presbyterian church. Dispatch had had a hard time deciphering the details, given the woman's state of mind. The upshot was definitely a body, and maybe a gator.

After letting dispatch know they were responding, Goff allowed a small smirk, which caused his silvery and rather impressive mustache to inch up toward his nostrils.

"That'd be the Buck Griffin Lake, I figure," he said. "And if she thinks she saw a gator in it, well, I got some land to sell her."

"Wouldn't be the first time a gator turned up where it wasn't wanted," Crenshaw said. He was originally from St. Pete, where, apparently, the gators were less respectful of their boundaries.

"That lake's man-made," Goff said with a huff. "It's in the middle of that park off Sixteenth. Nothing there to interest any gator."

"Well, if there is a gator, it could be real bad news. I see kids over there all the time," Crenshaw said. "Carol said the woman on the phone was really upset, talking about lots of blood."

Goff turned onto Forest Park Avenue, which ran the length of the west side of the park. He could see a few people clumped together in the grass on the right, where a concrete path led to the footbridge that connected a tree-filled promontory on the west side to a grassy one on the east.

"'A lot of blood' doesn't necessarily mean much when a civilian says it," Goff said. "Not compared to what you or I have seen."

He pulled the Sheriff's Office cruiser to the curb and ducked his head to squint through the windshield at the group that looked pretty relieved to see them. They were two men in their seventies or eighties and a woman of about the same age. The woman had one hand to her eyes. The other hand clutched the leash of some miniature designer dog.

"Well," he said, as he and Crenshaw unbuckled their seat belts. "Let's see what we got."

Goff slid out of the cruiser, stood up straight, and grabbed his overburdened belt to jerk up his pants. He was a blue-eyed, silver-haired wisp of a man who looked like a strong breeze could kick his ass, but this was a lie he had used to his advantage more than once.

Crenshaw had been discharged from the army over a year ago, but the military haircut, physique, and mannerisms stayed with him. He pulled a police issue AR-15 rifle from the gun lock between the cruiser's seats and slid out.

Abel Starkey trotted across the grass toward them. He was in his late seventies and just about as round as he was short, wearing a plaid button-up shirt on top and Birkenstocks on bottom. His khaki shorts met his white socks at his knees. Goff knew him enough to say hello to at the store.

"Hey there, Mr. Starkey," Goff said. "What we got goin' on over here?"

"He's down that way," Starkey said, pointing down the path. "He's on the bank over where the bridge starts."

"So, your wife's the one that saw the gator?" Deputy Crenshaw asked. Goff could see him trying not to have a facial expression. "She's not my wife, she's with my neighbor, Richard," Starkey said. "And I didn't see any gator. Just the body. She came running back to the house—me and Richard were having coffee—dragging her little hamster behind her and screaming about some guy that got killed by a gator. Come on, come talk to her."

"Starkey," Goff asked, as the two officers followed the old man. "You've been here a long time. You ever see an alligator in Buck Griffin Pond?"

"I been here since before there *was* a Buck Griffin Pond, and of course I've never seen a gator in it. But I never saw a dead guy, either."

They stopped in front of the older couple. The woman was sniffing into a man's handkerchief, and the dog was barking, his voice hoarse. Goff had little affection for puny dogs, and he guessed the thing had been barking since birth. He glared down at it, and it growled once for show, then shut up.

Unlike Starkey, the second old man looked like ribs and twigs wrapped up in crumpled brown paper. He was almost as skinny as Goff, though he had that peculiar round belly that skinny old men sometimes did.

"It's about time you got here," the second man cawed. "She's a mess. I need to get her back to the house."

"What's your name, sir?" Goff asked.

"King. Richard King," the man answered. He had a broad accent that Goff assumed was New York City, though he could have been from anywhere up north. They all sounded alike to him.

"And your wife here is the one that called in?"

The woman nodded, but King held up a liver-spotted hand. "She's not my wife, she's my girlfriend. She's visiting."

The woman blew her nose and lowered the hanky. She had almost-yellow dyed hair, and at this early hour, she was in full makeup. "Delores Burns," the woman said. Her hand trembled as she dabbed at her face.

Crenshaw repositioned himself to gain a better vantage on the glassy lake, adjusting his AR-15 with practiced ease. "So, you're the one that actually saw the gator?" His confidence with the rifle was counterbalanced by his disconcerted glances at the still water. Goff hadn't brought a rifle. Whether that was because he doubted they'd find a gator, or because he figured his wheel gun would be sufficient, Crenshaw didn't know.

"I didn't see the alligator, I just saw the man, the man's body," she answered, in an accent that was even thicker than her boyfriend's.

"She's from Jersey City, what does she know from gators?" King asked.

"I know what a body looks like! These, I've seen plenty," Delores snapped. "He's right there on the bank, half in the water, all bit up and bloody."

Goff jerked his head at Crenshaw. "Go have a look-see."

As Crenshaw moved off toward the bridge, Goff looked back at the clutch of old people. "So, nobody actually saw a gator."

"Never had no gators in the Buck Griffin," Starkey said, matter-of-fact.

"There's a canal goes in and out of the lake. Could have been a bull shark, even," King said.

"Reckon it could," Starkey affirmed. "Sometime back, this was way back, I think, we had us a big bull shark biting tourists all around here."

"Bull sharks are always biting tourists," King said with the authority of a transplant. "They're attracted to the coconut oil."

"This one I'm thinking of bit a bunch of tourists…all up an' down this stretch of sand," Starkey said, waving his arm in the general direction of the Gulf.

"Otis," Goff put in. "I remember him." He glanced off to his right as he saw Crenshaw coming back.

"Otis, that's the one! Damn near forgot what we called him," Starkey said.

"Well, there's a body down there," Crenshaw said. "White male."

"Of course, there's a body," King said. "That's what she just said."

"How's it look?" Goff asked.

"I didn't go any farther than the path," Crenshaw answered. "But it's messy."

"All right, call it in, and get some units over to the other side of the bridge to keep people from walkin' in," Goff said.

"We were just saying," King said. "Those bull sharks, they've been known to come inland, you know."

"Yeah, Otis came inland a time or two," Starkey added.

"Land shark, huh?" Crenshaw muttered as he headed for the cruiser.

"What are we, *schmucks*?" King asked Goff. "I said inland, not on land."

"Son of a gun was twelve feet long," Starkey continued, seeming oblivious to his friend's gripe. "Y'all want to see him, just head on down to Petie's Speakeasy on No Name Road out by The Kink. Pete's got him hanging on the wall."

"Reckon Otis has an alibi, then," Goff said.

Starkey glared. "But, Otis ain't the only bull shark," he said, "All I know is, if someone got bit in the Buck Griffin, it wasn't by some gator."

Goff sighed, perching his hands on his hips. "Listen, y'all. So far, we don't know for sure that anybody got bit by anything."

He looked around the park, all of it visible from where he stood. Thankfully, no one else was there. Too cold. Most likely, Cupcake, or whatever the snotty little dog was called, was the only reason Delores had been out.

He turned to look as he heard a vehicle behind him. It was a St. Joe PD cruiser. Sgt. Bill Knight climbed out, and Goff met him halfway.

"Heard you got a body," Knight said.

"Looks like," Goff answered. "Can you help us out with some officers to keep people out of the park? We've got more SO folks responding shortly, along with Crime Scene."

"Sure thing," Knight answered. "I'll get another couple of guys out here, over on 16th, and at either end. Where's your body?"

Goff jerked his head. "Down by the water, over where the bridge starts. You care to get these folks' contact information and send 'em home? I need to go have a look."

"Got it," Knight answered as he keyed his radio and walked away.

Goff looked over at Crenshaw, who was slamming the door of their cruiser. "Crenshaw, let's go have a look."

The two of them crossed the grassy area and then the Port City Trail, a scenic, ten-foot wide, paved path that ran parallel to the park and wound four miles through the city. This brought them to the concrete path that led to the bridge.

There weren't many trees in the park, and most of those were on the spit of land that jutted into the lake on this side. They stood on either side of the path, along with a decent amount of shrubbery, before the path opened onto the bridge.

The area at the foot of the bridge was completely open, all well-manicured grass. Goff and Crenshaw were still a good twenty feet from the bridge when Goff saw the first sign that they had a real problem on their hands. At the base of a mature tree, the last one before getting to the cleared area around the bridge, Goff spotted some matted grass and divots of dirt that looked like the scene of some kind of struggle, along with several large spots of blood. The spots led out past the trees, toward the lake.

Goff pointed at the blood, and Crenshaw nodded as they followed the trail but stayed well to the side of it. As they neared the area where the grass began to descend to the lake, Goff spotted a good deal more blood; on the grass, and on the rail at the end of the bridge. Goff walked close enough to see down the embankment, and there he saw a man facedown on the bank, his head and one shoulder in the yellowish water. The man was wearing a bright blue tracksuit and athletic shoes. There looked to be some blood staining on the back of the jacket, but Goff couldn't see any obvious source.

From where they stood, the coppery smell of blood tainted the cool air. Crenshaw scanned the shoreline for irregular shapes or threatening ripples. Nothing stirred but a few dragonflies. The park was silent, though off in the distance they heard sirens approaching.

"Maybe it *was* a shark," Crenshaw said half-seriously.

"If it was a shark, it must have been the walking kind," Goff snorted.

"Landshark?" Crenshaw asked, dubiously.

"Candygram," Goff said, in a childlike voice that the younger deputy barely recognized.

"What?"

"Candygram," Goff said. He looked like he was about to explain, but then just said, "Never mind. Guess you weren't born yet."

"Guess not," Crenshaw said. "Evan's probably gonna want to be called. I'm going to have to say it wasn't a shark *or* a gator that did this."

Goff blew a sigh through his mustache and hooked his thumbs over his utility belt. "Yep. If this was an animal attack, I'll eat the leftovers."

· ● ✳ ● ·

Sheriff Evan Caldwell had been standing in the same spot for almost ten minutes. Piggly-Wiggly had four shelves devoted to nothing but an amazing variety of cat food, and Evan had picked up and glared at almost every item. The handles of the red basket he held were starting to cut into his hand, laden as it was with coffee, bottled water, and a few navel oranges. With a sigh of exasperated resignation, he lowered the basket to the floor and picked up a can so small it looked like it was meant to feed Barbie's cat.

He spun it in his hand and frowned at the ingredients list. Okay, so the ingredients were all natural, but natural to whom? Since when did cats eat carrots or rice? In all his years of watching Wild Kingdom, he'd never seen a tiger sneak up on a patch of kale.

He slapped the can back down on the shelf, then looked up as he heard someone laugh. A red-haired woman in her late fifties was shaking her head at him. There were two bags of dry food and a pile of cans as well in her cart.

"You sure are giving it a lot of thought," she said, smiling as she gave him a discreet once-over. Six foot one, with nearly black hair, an abundance of long lashes, and bright green eyes, Evan got the once-over quite a bit, though he usually failed to notice. It used to be that Hannah would laugh later, and point it out to him. She also used to say that the thin white scar that ran from his lower lip to his chin was the only thing that saved him from being too pretty.

"I'm sorry?"

"The cat food. Are you looking for something in particular?" she asked him.

"Food, I guess," Evan said, shrugging one shoulder. "Something I actually want to buy that he'll actually want to eat."

"Picky, is he?" The woman nodded knowingly. Evan noticed she had a sticker on her purse that declared cat people to be happy people.

"He likes to throw up a lot," Evan said. "After reading these labels I can see why."

"Well, I don't buy it because it's too expensive for my blood, but these refrigerated ones are supposed to be the best," the woman said, gesturing at a small cooler behind her.

"Huh," Evan said, walking over to inspect the cooler. He opened the door and pulled out what looked like a tube of liverwurst. On the label, a very serene-looking cat sat on what was surely an organic field of grass. Evan turned it over to read the ingredients. "Lamb, chicken, chicken broth, sweet potatoes and rice."

"Yeah, all whole foods," the lady said.

Evan looked up at her. "But it's people food," he said. "I might as well just cook up a big batch of chicken for him."

"Well, can you cook up a batch for my brood, too? I've got five."

Evan almost shivered as he put the cat food back in the cooler. Five. He'd take a firing squad first. He smiled at the woman anyway.

"You must really like your cat," she said. "He's a lucky boy."

"He's a jerk," Evan said as she started to move along. "I just think it's ridiculous that I have to choose between chicken genitals and overpriced people food."

The woman's smile faltered just slightly, and Evan was about to think of something more acceptable to say when his cell phone rang. He shrugged at her like he was sorry to end their conversation and pulled it from his back pocket. The number told him it was his office assistant, Vi Hartigan.

He answered as he picked up his basket. "Caldwell," he said.

"This is Vi," Vi said, as she always did. Her voice reminded him of Bette Davis. Old Bette, without the fake accent.

"Hello, Vi."

"There's a body in the park over off of 16th Street," she intoned, sounding like she was reprimanding him for leaving his dead people lying around.

"What park?" he asked her, getting into the express line. He'd only been there a few months, and as small as Port St. Joe was, he wasn't quite an expert on local geography yet.

"It's just south of the office," Vi answered. "I'll text you the address for your GPS."

"Okay. Who's on scene?"

"Sgt. Goff and Deputy Crenshaw. Crime Scene is on the way and there are more officers *en route*."

"So, it's a homicide then?" Evan smiled at the teen-aged girl who was the cashier. She looked disconcerted.

"That would appear to be the case," Vi said.

"Okay, do me a favor; tell Goff I'll be there in five."

"Thank you," Vi said, and hung up.

Evan paid for his purchases and carried both bags in one hand as he exited the store. He stopped just a few yards outside the door, pulled his cigarettes from his other pants pocket and lit one.

He sucked in a lungful, then exhaled slowly into the chilly, damp air. He'd intended to try to take the day off, but he had to admit that he was relieved he had something more definite to do. He caught a glimpse of himself in the reflection of his vehicle and really wished he could justify going home to put on one of his suits. Instead, he tossed his bags in the back seat, then tucked his blue chambray shirt into his tan cargo pants. That would have to do.

TWO

EVAN PULLED OUT of the Pig's lot, heading east on Marina Drive, then hooked a right onto Monument Avenue. Out the passenger side window, the Gulf sparkled in the dazzling morning sun, reflecting back, in deeper hues, the blue of the cloudless sky.

The salt water called to him, as it always did, but he wouldn't be able to take that call today. He had not, in fact, been out on the Gulf in almost a month. He'd been telling himself he was too busy to take the boat out. His life had been turned inside out in recent months. He'd moved across the state from bustling Brevard County, his wife was in a long-term nursing facility, his new, or former new, boss was dead, and he'd been shoved into the role of acting Sheriff.

The pressures of the new job, the care of his wife, his sense of displacement in his new home, and the fallout from his former boss's suicide all colluded to fill every waking moment with tasks and calls and visits and a sense of perpetual incompletion.

The demanding workload of his personal life and his professional responsibilities provided a reasonable excuse for his absence from the water, the one place he always felt at home. Evan knew if he kept telling himself he hadn't taken the boat out because he just didn't have time, eventually he would accept that answer. He also knew he'd never really believe it. The true reason was deeper, a profound sense of failure, a sense that he didn't deserve the peace that a day, or even a few hours, on the water would grant him.

Sheriff Randy Hutchens had been loved and well respected by all residents of Gulf County, with a few notable exceptions. He had been heavily involved in the schools, especially the high school football program. His sudden death had devastated the community and had thrust Evan into the unenviable position of replacing him. All that had been bad enough, but as the circumstances of Hutch's death surfaced, things took a turn for the terrible.

Hutch had been the type of man that some local author would probably write a book about. Not that anyone outside Gulf County would actually read that book, but his constituents thought of him as a significant part of their history. At least, they had before it came to light that he had been a long-time wife beater. Before it came to light that he had coerced a slow, but inherently sweet, petty criminal to shoot him in the back of the head so that he could portray his suicide as a death in the line of duty.

Now, that petty criminal, Tommy Morrow, was facing a choice between life in prison or life in prison awaiting the electric chair. Hutch's widow, Marlene, who vehemently denied that her husband ever raised a hand to her, had at first gone on the offensive against the Sheriff's Office, and Evan in particular, telling anyone who would listen that the wife-beater/suicide story was a cover-up concocted to hide … something. She never quite stated what it was she believed was being covered up. Eventually, she realized what everybody else had known from her first statements, that her angry rants were part of her grieving process and that nobody believed her conspiracy theory.

A few days after Hutch was laid to rest, Marlene disappeared without a word to anyone. Evan learned that she had moved to Pensacola to stay with her daughter and son-in-law. The Sheriff's Office was unable to pay the line of duty death benefit, and she had been left with the moderate life insurance payout. Evan had wanted to do something for her, a community benefit or even just passing the hat among Sheriff's Department Employees, but Vi had advised against it.

She left town because she was angry and embarrassed. You send her anything other than prayers and she's going to be even more angry and even more embarrassed, Vi had told him. Evan was not responsible for any of the drama or tragedy that these people had experienced, but he had been the one to discover it. To some of the people in the Gulf County Sheriff's Office, and to some of Gulf County's residents, Evan was now the face of their sorrow and confusion.

He wondered, as he navigated the light traffic on Monument, as he had been wondering for the past two months, whether he had done the right thing. He wondered if there was anything else he *could* have done. In difficult situations, the easy choice and the right choice never seem to be the same choice.

An idea had come to Evan in the wake of his wife's accident, one he now considered a truth, the idea that pain and fear are not the enemy. Pain and fear define the human condition, and to live a life without at least a passing acquaintance with either is to be less than human. *Flinch forward*, some grizzled veteran officer had told him once, years ago when Evan was a rookie. *These macho guys try to train themselves not to flinch, that's stupid. God gave you that reflex to keep you alive. Something scares you, lean into it, not away.* Flinch forward. *As soon as you retreat from fear or hurt, they gotcha. Might as well pull up your traps and call it a day.*

Evan looked right again, toward the gleam of the sun on the water. He'd spent all of his forty years on the Atlantic, but if it was salt water, he was drawn to it.

Overhead, a squadron of pelicans patrolled the coast-line in close formation.

The image Hutch had constructed for himself and his personal beliefs were at odds with his own truth. The picture he had painted of his life was a lie, but it was a lie far too valuable to destroy. If Hutch had ever decided to become the man he wanted to believe he was, he would have had to admit to himself how far out of sync with that ideal his life had drifted. And that admission was either too painful, or too frightening. A bullet in the head, and whatever waited for him after, had seemed easier.

Evan felt that familiar hollow wanting to open up in the pit of his gut, that sensation telling him he was tread-ing too close to his own terrifying truths. He inhaled deeply, filling his lungs with salt air and smoke.

Lean into it, he thought.

A horn blared behind him. He shot a glance at his rearview. A large, white vehicle loomed there, briefly, before shooting into the oncoming lane of traffic. Tires squealed on asphalt. As it blew past him, Evan recog-nized the Medical Examiner's van. Dr. Mitch Grundy, the M.E. himself, liked to drink. More often than not, he sent interns out to do his job.

Evan pulled the cigarette out of his mouth. It was almost down to a nub, anyway. Just as he decided to snub it in his ashtray, but before he actually did, the M.E.'s van swerved back over into his lane, narrowly avoiding a head-on with an oncoming minivan. Evan grabbed the wheel with both hands and stomped on the brake pedal. The cigarette vanished. The van missed Evan's front bumper by inches, then rocketed down the road, hooking a left on 16th.

Evan followed the van. Five blocks up the road, he arrived at Forest Park South, also known as Buck Griffin Lake. An acrid smell tickled his nostrils. He scanned the floorboards but didn't see the cigarette. Then, a thin tendril of smoke caught his eye. He followed it to its source to find the cigarette, now finally extinguished, resting on the toe of his left shoe. His favorite deck shoes. It had burned a tear-shaped black blister in the brown leather. He cursed softly as he rolled through the lot to where Grundy had parked.

The Medical Examiner's van slanted across three spaces, slightly lopsided because its right front tire was up on the curb. Evan expected to see Mitch Grundy stumble out the door and pretend to be sober. It would be nice to finally have a face to put with the name. He thought about calling Trigg to ask her to grab a cup of black coffee on her way in but decided against it. He figured he was more likely to throw it in the doctor's face than let him drink it.

He needed to remain calm. Grundy was a poor excuse for an M.E. – a poor excuse for a man, as far as Evan was concerned – but if you need to pound nails and all you have is a rock, well, you use a rock. Evan didn't guess he'd do his job any better with a broken nose.

He pulled into a parking space, just one, next to the van and got out. The van's door swung open, and Evan was surprised to see not Dr. Grundy, but one of his interns, Danny Coyle, hop out. He was a tall, lanky kid in his mid-twenties, and Evan thought him an odd blend of geek and hipster, with his slightly shaggy black hair and his black-rimmed glasses.

Danny had the metabolism of a nervous squirrel, though perhaps not the attention span. But his enthusiasm for his work and his surprising competence had earned him more respect than a kid his age typically acquired. Evan was still chapped that Grundy had sent an intern to do his work for him, but he was also relieved.

"You nearly put me in the ditch back there, Coyle," Evan said. He couldn't quite muster the anger he had just been trying to suppress.

"Oh, sorry Sheriff, I didn't realize that was you, right?" Danny said, so quickly that it almost sounded like a single syllable. "I just didn't want to be the last one on scene again. You guys gave me hell about it last time."

Evan pursed his lips and nodded. "I assume Dr. Grundy had pressing business elsewhere?"

"Oh, yeah, he's otherwise occupied," Coyle said earnestly. "Besides, it's Saturday. Bosses don't show up on Saturdays."

"I'm here," Evan said, lighting a new cigarette.

"Well, yeah, but you're always here. Or there, as the case may be, right?" Coyle said, pulling a black plastic case and a large duffle from the van.

Evan cocked his head as he waited for his hearing to catch up with Danny's speaking.

"You know, I've heard some people around here think you work too much."

"And these people," Evan asked, "they have all of their affairs in order to the point that they have time to worry about mine?"

He started walking briskly toward the gathering crowd of deputies. The kid grabbed a huge vat of a travel mug from his console before slamming the door and running to catch up.

Evan eyed the dark purple liquid sloshing around in Danny's hand. He pointed at the tumbler. "So, what is it this morning?

"Oh, this is probably my most mind-blowing combo to date," Danny said at the speed of light. "Beets, celery, cucumber, kale, lemon, and ginger." He held it out to Evan. "Try a sip. It'll jerk you right out of your shoes, right?"

Evan smiled but shook his head. He considered himself a nutrition snob, despite his smoking, but he preferred to chew his food. "I don't doubt your claim, but maybe some other time."

"I really encourage you to start juicing, Sheriff," Danny said as they approached the crime scene. "It's like freebasing all those vitamins and phytonutrients. You'll never drink coffee again."

That thought made Evan want to weep. "I'm sure it's great," he said anyway. "But I live on a boat. I don't even have room for an electric can opener."

"Ah," Danny said, nodding and frowning like Evan was being oppressed. "Bothersome."

THREE

GOFF AND CRENSHAW HAD hung yellow
tape from the bridge, around the trees, and down to
the embankment. Several bright yellow plastic trian-
gles, numbered in black, perched in the grass around
the trees, and closer to the bridge. These marked where
evidence was or had been. It looked to Evan like these
were marking several areas of blood spatter and pooling.

Crenshaw stood with several other deputies in a loose
huddle. Evan slipped under the crime scene tape and
went to stand near the group of officers.

"Hey, boss," Crenshaw said.

"Crenshaw," Evan said, nodding to include everyone. "Gentlemen."

From where he now stood, he could see Goff down
on the embankment, talking to Paula Trigg, Gulf County's crime scene investigator. Trigg had put up a white
plastic screen that surrounded the body on three sides,

but that wasn't deterring the looky-loos much. Across the lake, in the street that ran along the other length of the park, several people pointed their phones at the scene. He looked over at a thick-necked, blond deputy named Holland. "Let's see if we can keep this from turning into a sideshow," he said, nodding at the crowd.

At one time, the media was Evan's only concern when it came to information or images being made public that shouldn't have been. Now, anyone with a cell phone was a potential problem. Evan had no time or taste for social media; he only had a Facebook page because his more social, event-planner wife had created one. The only posts on it were the ones she had shared, and those had stopped over a year ago.

Holland eyed him coolly. He was one of a handful of deputies who hadn't yet warmed up to Evan. He opened his mouth, closed it, then turned to the two guys next to him. "You heard the man. Crenshaw, you got more of that tape?"

Crenshaw did. He and the other officers left to send the onlookers back to their homes and expand the perimeter to include the streets that bordered the park.

"Can I go on down?" Danny asked. Evan had forgotten he was standing next to him.

"No, it looks like Trigg is still taking pictures," Evan answered. "Give me a minute. Why don't you go keep warm in the van? I'll call you when we're ready."

The kid looked like he'd just been told he couldn't go out to play. "Yeah, okay," he said, and turned to head back the way they'd come.

Evan made his way down the embankment, stepping wide of any evidence markers. Goff and Trigg turned to him and waited. Paula Trigg was a local who'd gone to Miami for college and stayed for another fifteen years to work with Miami-Dade PD. She didn't talk about her time in Miami too much, but Evan knew that she and her K-9 partner had been ambushed by three Columbians who did dirty work for a local dealer. Trigg and her partner, Eddie, had both been shot, the dog losing a leg. The Columbians didn't make it. Ernie had gotten one, and Paula had shot the other two. Once they'd both recovered, Trigg had been allowed to adopt the dog, and they'd both moved back to Gulf County.

Trigg was striking more than she was pretty, with dark hair cut in a severe bob and sharp, high cheekbones that hinted at a Native American branch to the family tree. Their shared love of Cuban food and *café con leche* was as personal as they got, but she was whip-smart and occasionally funny and Evan liked her.

"Got a call about a gator attack," Goff said as Evan approached.

"It was a gator?" Evan asked.

"Not unless it was a gator with thumbs," Paula said.

"The gal that called it in just saw a bunch of blood and a body by the water and assumed gator," Goff said. "She's from New York City."

"What do we know so far?" Evan asked, looking down at the body.

"Not a heap," Goff answered. "No ID in his back pocket and we haven't moved him yet. Trigg just finished her first pictures of him. We were getting ready to turn him over. But looks like white male, late thirties to early forties. Tracksuit, watch, and a wedding ring."

"Judging by the blood pool underneath the body, we can assume our COD is in the front," Trigg said.

"Lot of blood up there," Evan said. "So, I'm guessing whatever happened to this guy happened up near the path."

"Right. Also, given the flattened grass coming down this way, and the fairly even, intermittent bloodstains, I'm guessing he rolled down here," Trigg stated. "Whether he was pushed down or just fell and rolled on his own, I don't know."

"You ready to turn him over?" Evan asked.

"Yeah," Trigg answered, handing him her camera. "Goff, can you give me a hand?"

Goff and Trigg squatted on either side of the body and slowly rolled him onto his back. The victim's limbs flopped loosely as they turned him. The guy hadn't been dead long.

"Hellfire," Goff said quietly. "Somebody did a number on him."

Someone had. The entire front of the man's jacket was a chaos of blood and fissure. The holes and tears seemed to be concentrated on his right side, just under his breast.

Trigg held her hand out for her camera, and after handing it to her, Evan reached into his pocket for the blue disposable gloves he'd grabbed from his glove compartment. Trigg and Goff were already gloved up. Evan's pack of Marlboros fell out of his pocket, and Trigg glanced over as he bent to retrieve it.

"I beg of you, don't light up anywhere around me today," Trigg said. "I quit smoking."

"When?" Evan asked, pulling on his gloves.

"Eleven hours ago, if you count eight hours of sleeping." Trigg started taking pictures of the body.

"I quit for six years. The first five days are like crawling through Hell on your hands and knees, but it gets easier after that," Evan said.

Trigg threw him a look. "Thanks for the pep talk."

Goff and Evan stood out of her way while she took shots from both a standing and a crouching position, then she stood and nodded at Evan. He and Goff both squatted down.

"All these entrance wounds and no exits," Evan mused. "Clearly knife over gun."

He lifted the man's jacket and the white undershirt beneath it. Goff whistled as they saw several narrow wounds. Many of them overlapped, making it difficult to count how many there actually were. That would be a job for Danny.

"Overkill," Trigg said without humor.

"Yeah. Somebody was pissed," Evan replied.

The man was wearing a runner's belt; the kind with a zipper all the way across, meant to hold keys, a wallet, and anything else somebody wanted to bring along to the gym or on a run. Evan could see the clear outline of a cell phone.

He unzipped the belt and reached inside, pulled out a Samsung phone. He used an iPhone and wasn't up on Androids, but it was one of the larger models, probably fairly new. There were three text messages pinned to the screen, all from someone named Karen. The earliest was from just after seven.

7:08 am Hey babe you need to hurry. Softball practice at 8.

7:42 am Where are u?

7:51 am dammit never mind

"Crap," Evan said quietly. He handed the phone to Goff. "Don't bag that just yet."

He reached into the belt and pulled out the only other two items: a ten-dollar bill and a Florida driver's license. The victim looked somewhat more cheerful in the photo, but it was clearly him. Jake William Bellamy, aged thirty-nine, five-nine and one hundred-fifty pounds. His address was listed as Juniper Avenue. Evan knew that one; it was about half a mile south of the park. He'd looked at a rental there when he'd first moved from Cocoa Beach. Evan noticed the license was a new one, issued just three weeks earlier.

He pulled out his phone and texted the address to himself, then handed the license to Trigg, who dropped it into an evidence bag and started labeling it. Evan reached over to pick up the man's right wrist, turning it slightly. There was a through and through puncture in the palm, along with a shallow slice. There were other cuts on both wrists and the back of the left hand.

"Guy put up a real fight," Goff muttered sympathetically.

"Looks like," Evan replied. "Trigg, make sure you bag his hands. Maybe he scratched the guy."

He looked up to see her glaring down at him indignantly. "Sorry, Paula. I know I don't need to tell you how to do your job. Just thinking out loud."

He looked up at Goff. "Get the number for those text messages, would you, Goff? And see if there were any outgoing calls or texts this morning. Or when the last one was."

Evan looked up at Paula. "Did you look around for a weapon?"

"We looked within a twenty-five-yard radius, that's it," she answered. "Newman and Frye are looking further afield right now."

"We'll want to check the water," Evan said. "Killer could have tossed it from the embankment or the bridge. Any idea how deep this is?"

"No. Probably just enough to be a pain in the butt. It's murky as hell, too."

Evan nodded, then straightened up. He looked at Goff.

"No outgoing calls today. No incoming any more recent than just after eleven last night." Goff looked up from the phone. "Some guy named Roy."

"Okay, go ahead and bag it," Evan said. He looked at Paula. "You ready for Danny?"

"I'm never ready for Danny," she answered.

"I thought you liked the kid," Evan said.

"I do. I might even invite him over for a barbecue sometime, if it's okay with his mom," she said. "But his energy level is a little overwhelming."

Goff made some sort of indeterminate noise underneath his mustache.

"Understood," Evan said.

"He can come on," Paula said with a sigh. She'd taken a few pictures once they'd turned the body over, but they'd rely on Danny's photographs during autopsy for photo documentation of any wounds.

"I'll get him," Goff said.

Evan held up a hand. "I'll tell him," he said, standing. "I need to have a—" He caught Trigg's scowl. "I need to stretch."

"Yeah, stretch one for me, too," Paula snapped as he walked away.

· ● ✳ ● ·

Evan had to pass a Sheriff's Office cruiser on his way to Danny's van. Deputies Ginny Frances and Frank DuPree were standing at the hood of the cruiser, a donut box between them.

"Hey, boss," Ginny said, lifting the box. "You want the last donut?"

"Seriously? What kind of stereotypes bring donuts to a crime scene?" Evan asked, trying not to grin.

"The kind that were at Dunkin' Donuts when they got the call," DuPree answered.

"What flavor is it?" Evan asked as he pulled his cigarettes from his pocket.

"Glazed," Ginny answered.

"I'll pass, but I'll take it to Danny," Evan said. He lit up and blew out a puff of smoke as Ginny wrapped the donut in a napkin and handed it to him.

"You get an ID, yet?" Ginny asked.

"Yeah, but I need to get the kid situated before we notify," Evan answered. "Hopefully, we'll still get to the family before the press moves in."

"Channel Four's down at the corner already," DuPree said.

"I saw," Evan said. The news van was several hundred yards away, behind the cruisers parked across Marvin Avenue. "Do me a favor. Radio those officers and tell them to keep their eyes on those guys. Nobody slips into our crime scene."

"Shoot to kill?" Ginny asked as Evan walked off.

"If provoked."

Danny was slouched in the driver's seat, his face oddly aglow. Evan puzzled over this for a moment. Then he noticed the source of the strange illumination, an iPad Mini tucked into the van's instrument panel, behind the steering wheel. A TV show was playing. It made Evan smile in spite of himself.

He tapped on the window. Danny looked over at him, a bit surprised, but not startled. He rolled down his window.

"What are you watching?" Evan asked him.

"*Dexter!*" the kid answered enthusiastically.

"That's a cop show, right?"

"Marginally," Danny answered, pausing the show. "Forensics guy in Miami, right, who also happens to be a serial killer who kills serial killers."

"Okay," Evan said flatly. "Homework, then?"

Danny laughed. "Extra credit, right?"

Evan held up the donut. "We're ready for you. I brought you a snack."

"Oh, thanks Sheriff Caldwell," Danny said, poking his head out the window. His tone was full of genuine gratitude, but then he added, "Is that certified organic?"

"Yes, Danny," Evan said without hesitation. "This is a certified, free-range, non-GMO, fat-free, gluten free, sugar-free, truth free, deep fried and heavily frosted doughnut. Last one in the box."

Danny peered at the donut suspiciously. "I usually only eat sweets on the last day of the month."

Evan squinted at the kid as he blew a mouthful of smoke in the other direction. Then the kid winked at him.

"I had you going there for a minute, didn't I?" Danny asked, getting out of the van.

"Sure, you had me going. Acting's easy when you're playing yourself."

"I don't get it," Danny said, turning to pull his bags back out of the van.

"You and your liquid diet," Evan replied. "You want the donut, or do I need to chew it for you first?"

Danny plucked the donut from Evan's hand. "Thanks!"

Evan gave the kid credit; the donut was gone before they arrived back down to Goff, Trigg, and Mr. Bellamy. When they got there, Goff was holding evidence bags open while Trigg snipped at clumps of grass with a pair of what looked like cuticle scissors.

"Zowie," Danny said quietly as he saw the body. "Poor guy."

Goff and Trigg stood.

"Anything new?" Evan asked.

"No," Trigg answered, blowing her bangs out of her eyes. "If the victim managed to draw any blood when he was trying to fight this guy off, it's probably up there by the trees, but I'm grabbing some of this anyway."

"I need to go notify the family," Evan said wearily. "I'll be back shortly, Danny, to see what preliminary findings you come up with."

"Sure, yeah," the kid said, opening his voluminous duffel.

Just then a few bars of a familiar song sounded from somewhere near Evan's feet. It took a moment for him to place it as the theme from *Sesame Street*. Trigg bent over her evidence bag on the grass and pulled out the baggie containing Bellamy's ringing phone, the display lit up in cheerful, bright blue.

"Oh, geez," Trigg said, as the ringing stopped. She handed the baggie to Evan. The phone showed a missed call from Danielle, and two text messages from a few minutes earlier.

9:18 am Mom's really mad you missed practice.

9:19 am But I caught a fly ball!! followed by a multitude of emojis.

Evan sighed, as Goff read over his shoulder and clucked his tongue. He handed the bag back to Trigg.

"I need to get over there," he said quietly.

"You want me to come with?" Goff asked.

Evan looked at Trigg.

"Yeah, take him," Trigg said. "I'll get Crenshaw to help me out."

Goff was silent as he followed Evan back up the embankment. Evan was in his own head. He hated notifications anyway, but when kids were involved, it was especially hard.

When their feet hit the sidewalk, Ginny Frances called out, a white bundle in her hand.

"Hey, Ruben!" she said to Goff. "Saved you a Boston Cream."

They veered that way, and Goff took the donut. "Thanks, Ginny."

Ginny caught Evan's eye and shrugged defensively. "They're his favorite," she said.

Evan wanted to toss out a good line, but the mood wasn't there, and he was having trouble thinking of anything to say. He strode to his car, Goff's boots clumping behind him. As little as he weighed, Evan was surprised his boots made noise.

Evan pulled open his door and got in. Goff slipped in as Evan was starting the car. He popped the last of his donut into his mouth as Evan cranked on the heat. There was a gob of custard on the bottom of his mustache.

"Every time I do a next of kin, I think about retiring," Goff said.

"Me, too," Evan said. "You've got, what, thirty years?"

"Thirty-two," Goff answered.

"That's a lot for a cop," Evan said. "Why don't you do it?"

Goff shrugged. "Got a few years left on the mortgage," he said.

Evan surveyed the park and the flurry of activity around the little bridge. He thought about years and mortgages and next of kin, and still did not know what to say. When he turned back to Goff, he said the first thing that came to mind, "You've got custard on your mustache."

As Evan pulled out of the parking spot, Goff answered, "Saving that for the missus."

FOUR

IT TOOK ONLY a few minutes to reach the Bellamy home. In a neighborhood of fairly new, middle-class homes, it was a tastefully bland single-story house with attached, two-car garage and a manicured lawn. The garage door was open. It contained a black Chrysler sedan and a red Volkswagen minivan, both fairly new, and a collection of kids' bicycles and Little Tykes cars, all well-used.

A path of stone pavers led from the driveway to the front entrance, where a red door broke up the monotony of the house's façade. A large potted hibiscus sat next to the door.

Evan and Goff waited silently in Evan's vehicle for just a moment. Eventually, Goff said, "Well, I'm the one that found him. I guess it's only right that I do the notification."

"No," Evan said, opening his door. "It's my job. I'll do it."

"I'll let you."

They walked up the paved path. The home and grounds radiated a sense of pleasant perfection, nice without trying too hard. Evan doubted it would do anything to shield its occupants from the reality of a chaotic and pitiless world.

He pressed the glowing button beside the door. A faint melody sang out somewhere within. This was followed by the excited voices of young children. Evan waited, but no one came. He rapped his knuckles against the trim. This time, when he heard the children, their voices were quieter, as if they had been moved farther back in the house. But, still, no one answered.

Evan was about to knock again when the door eased open, just a crack at first, then a little more. The woman behind it looked terrified. She was probably in her late thirties, blonde and pretty, but her face was so drawn with worry that she looked much older. She had not disengaged the chain and now looked at Evan and Goff while taking refuge behind the door.

"Good morning, ma'am," Evan began, "Are you Mrs. Bellamy?"

She was already biting her bottom lip, turning its pale pink into a thin white line. Her lower eyelids were filling with tears as she nodded her head. Evan had his shield attached to his belt and Goff was in full uniform. Evan knew she already knew that her weekend wasn't going to be anything like she'd expected.

"Ma'am, my name is Sheriff Evan Caldwell, and this is Sgt. Goff. We're from the Gulf County Sheriff's Office," Evan explained. "May we come in and have a word with you?"

"Where's Jake?" she asked in a tiny voice.

"That's what we need to talk to you about, ma'am," Evan said gently, "but I think it would be better to do that inside. May we come in?"

Evan watched her eyes. He could never predict how an individual would react when notified that a loved one had died. A wild anger flashed across her face, but was gone as quickly as it had appeared, then the look of defeated terror was back. She nodded again, and one of the tears that had been poised on her eyelid slid down to her upper lip.

She undid the chain, then turned her back on them, leaving the door to hang open. There was a living room immediately to their right, and Goff quietly closed the front door before they followed her into it. She sat down on an overstuffed ivory couch in a pale green room. Ceiling fans, fashioned to look like white palm fronds, spun noiselessly overhead, helping the HVAC unit distribute the heated air.

Karen Bellamy stared at the driftwood coffee table as the two men took seats in a pair of green-striped chairs across from the couch. The children were nowhere to be seen, but Evan heard their voices from somewhere deeper in the house.

Evan took a breath and was about to speak when Mrs. Bellamy looked up at him.

"How bad is it?" she asked.

"Mrs. Bellamy," Evan started, "May I call you Karen?"

She nodded, then pulled her lips together. She didn't need to ask how he knew her first name; he knew because her world had imploded somewhere between dawn and softball practice.

"Karen, I am very sorry—"

She covered her mouth as a moan struggled for egress, then folded over and put her face on her knees.

"Oh, please God…"

Evan waited a moment as she drew in a couple of loud breaths, her face still hidden.

"I'm terribly sorry," Evan continued quietly. "It appears someone attacked your husband in the park just north of here. He was found around eight this morning. He had already died when he was found."

Karen sat up quickly, her face shifting with lightning speed from agony to adamancy. "I'm sorry," she said, "I don't understand what you're trying to say, but my husband—I think you've made a mistake. My husband just went running."

"Karen," Evan said, slowly and precisely, "your husband, Jake Bellamy, was killed this morning." He nodded his head and watched her eyes. "Jake is dead, Karen."

She shook her head, but Evan could see that she heard him. She turned to Goff, appealing like he had come to give her different, better news.

"I'm awfully sorry for your loss, ma'am," Goff said gently, heading her off.

She looked at him for several heartbeats, the emotions on her face seeming to shift with each. Finally, she spoke very slowly, "I...I understand... what you're saying, but... but you might be wrong, right? You must be mistaken. It's not him."

Goff pulled the evidence bag containing Bellamy's license out of his shirt pocket. He set it lightly down on the table in front of her. "This is the man that was found, ma'am. It's him."

The two men watched as her face changed by feature and in lightning-fast increments. Her tightly closed lips opened, her lower lip began to tremble. Fixed on the license, her eyes went from desperate to a dawning acceptance, and Evan watched as a tear dropped onto her right knee, making a darker circle of blue on her faded jeans.

Evan wanted to lean forward and offer her some kind of comfort, but it was too soon, he was too much a stranger, and he had nothing of real meaning to say. It would be up to the people she loved, the people who loved her, to give comfort.

He and Goff were there, present with her, and nothing else they could have done or said would be more than that. They sat and watched for her to be ready to hear more.

Evan had been in a serious car accident once, an accident that had given him the thin, white scar that ran from lip to chin. This kind of news was like that experience, the instant of impact is carved into the memory forever. The moments that follow are blank. At some point, clarity returns followed reluctantly by rational thought.

When Karen finally looked back up at them, the wildly fluctuating emotions had calmed, replaced by a dazed and vacant expression. Tears plastered a lock of hair to one cheek. She twisted her hands in her lap and stared at a spot between Goff and Evan.

"Mrs. Bellamy," Evan said, in his gentlest voice, "Can I call someone for you?"

She slowly turned her head to him.

"Do you have family or a close friend in town?" Evan tried again. "Someone I can call to come be with you?"

Her face tried to convulse into sobs again, but she held it back, clenching her jaw and covering her face with one hand. After a moment, she nodded her head in the affirmative.

"My mom," she choked out, "in Panama City." She pulled her phone from a pocket and thrust it at Evan. "But, but I... I can't..."

It took a few tries, but Evan managed to get the code from her and unlocked the phone. He found the listing for "Mom," then handed the phone back to her. She shook her head.

"Would you like me to call her, Karen?"

She nodded quickly, then rubbed at her wet upper lip.

Evan copied the number onto his keypad and was about to dial when they heard children's voices approaching from down the hall.

"Oh, the kids!" Karen said, covering her mouth. "No!"

Goff was up and into the hallway before she'd finished speaking. Two little girls stopped short. One looked to be about eight and was wearing a pink softball mitt. The other was younger, maybe five, and was mostly wearing a look of surprise.

"Oh, good, there y'all are," Goff said. "Your mama was just sending me to see if you'd take me to the kitchen to get a drink of water."

The older girl looked around Goff to the living room. Their mother was looking the other way. Evan nodded and smiled.

"You are a policeman," the younger girl said.

"I am," Goff answered.

"Is he the police, too?" The older girl asked.

"Yep, that's my boss, and he's visiting with your mom for a few minutes." Goff put a hand on each girl's shoulder and started herding them back down the hall. "Can y'all come help me get a drink?"

"Why are police here?" the older girl asked.

"Is the kitchen this way?" Goff asked as they came to the end of the hall.

"That way," the younger girl answered, though Goff could see it.

They walked into a white kitchen made almost painfully bright by the sunlight streaming through a sliding glass door in the breakfast nook.

"The water comes out of the 'frigerator door," the smaller girl said. She pointed at a big stainless fridge, the kind with the drawer in the bottom, like Goff's beautiful bride had been asking for. He'd been saving. He walked around the island, still steering the girls along with him.

"Can one of you fetch a glass for me?" he asked cheerfully.

The older girl opened a dishwasher door and pulled out a plastic souvenir tumbler that reminded the drinker of the great time they had during Christmas 2017 at Epcot.

"Thank you," Goff said quietly. "What's your name?"

"Danielle Marie," the girl answered, picking at her mitt.

"I'm Lauren," her sister volunteered.

Goff nodded at Danielle's mitt. "Looks like you play softball," he said, as he tried to figure out how to make the water go.

Danielle reached up and pushed an icon that lit up in blue. The water started dispensing.

"Yes, sir," she said.

"Me, too!" Goff said. She looked up at him, her brows knit together. "I play on the Sheriff's team. What position do you play?"

"Third base," she said. "What do you play?"

"Shortstop. Don't let the gray hair fool you, sugar. I'm quicker than Quaker Oats."

He sat down on one of the stools at the granite-covered island.

"Did Mommy get a ticket?" Danielle asked.

"No," Goff answered lightly.

"Is she in trouble?"

"Naw, nothing like that, Danielle Marie."

"Is Daddy in trouble?" the little one asked.

"No, honey, nobody's in trouble. My boss is just visiting your mama."

"Daddy's late," Danielle said flatly.

Goff nodded, looking at the fridge. "Hey, who drew that tiger there?" he asked, although he could clearly see Danielle's name on it.

"Me," she said. "Mrs. Newman entered it in the school art show."

"You don't say," Goff told her. "I can't draw a thing."

She looked back at him. "Daddy's late," she repeated.

Goff tried to look like a nice man who'd just stopped in to visit and get some water. "Is he now?" he asked.

"He missed my fly ball," she said.

Goff nodded. "Well, I'm sure he didn't mean to," he told her quietly.

· ● ✳ ● ·

Evan spent only a minute or two on the phone with Karen Bellamy's mother, who struck him as someone he would want notified in case of his own emergency. One gasp, a couple of quick and to-the-point questions, and she announced clearly, if a bit shakily, that she would be there within ninety minutes. It was she who suggested that Evan call the Bellamys' pastor, which he did after getting the name from Karen. He sounded younger than Evan supposed he expected and advised Evan that he would be there in twenty minutes.

Other than her pastor's name, Karen said nothing at all while Evan made the calls. She stared at her husband's driver's license on the table, or out the window behind Evan, to the inconsiderately sunny day. Evan pulled his small, black notebook and a pen from his pocket. It was only after Evan told her the minister was on his way that Karen met his eye again.

"Where is he?" she asked. "Jake?"

Evan hesitated a moment. "He's still at the park. We're still processing the scene."

She looked around quickly, then made as though to rise. Evan held up a hand.

"Karen, you can't be there," he said firmly. "I absolutely understand your instinct to be with him, but you need to let us do our work, okay? As soon as he's taken to the medical examiner's office you'll be allowed to see him if you want to."

He caught the slight flinch when he'd said the word, 'see.'

"Maybe...do I need to identify him?"

"No."

"Wait. What exactly happened to him?" She shook her head. "When you first told me, for some reason, I just thought that he was hit by a car, even though I heard what you said." She blinked a few times. "I mean, when you came to the door, that's what I expected, because what else would happen to him?"

"I understand. I'm sorry, but it appears he was attacked."

She covered her mouth for a moment, then shook her head. "This doesn't even seem real."

"It might take a while for everything to sink in," Evan told her. "Let it happen the way your mind wants it to. What time did your husband leave the house this morning?"

"Um, around six. He used to run a lot, but he was just getting back into it since we moved. He was trying to get healthier. He thought this was a good place for us to get out more, be more active."

"Did he run often?"

"Well, he's only gotten onto any kind of real sched-ule in the last few weeks or so. But he usually runs three times a week. Saturday mornings at six, and whichever couple of weeknights he got home early enough."

"Did he always run in the park over on Forest Park Road? I'm sorry, I don't actually know the name of the little park."

"I don't, either, although we've gone over there a couple of times to hang out and feed the coots while Jake ran." She blinked a few times, thinking. "I know he picked up that trail a couple of blocks over that way," she said, pointing east.

"The Port City Trail."

"Right. He took that up to the park, ran around the park, and came back the same way. He was trying to build up to running the whole trail. Four miles I think?"

The guy had almost gotten there. Evan was a long-time runner and had run the trail a few times, though he preferred to run near the water, closer to the marina.

"And he'd been running this route for a few weeks?"

"Yeah, something like that. I mean, he only started going all the way to the park a couple of weeks ago, maybe?"

Evan nodded. "Okay. And he never mentioned anyone that was maybe out of place on his runs, anyone that seemed off to him in any way?"

"No," she answered, shaking her head.

Evan took a deep breath as he watched her take a few of her own. "Karen, is there anyone you can think of who would want to hurt your husband? Anyone you know?"

"No! No, of course not," she said. "We're just regular people. We don't have enemies or drama or whatever. We don't even know that many people here yet."

"Are you new to the area?"

"Yes. Yes, we moved here right after Thanksgiving. Thanksgiving weekend. From Tallahassee."

"What brought you here?" Evan asked, taking notes.

"Jake was offered a transfer," she answered, staring out the window. "It was more money, and we've always talked about moving somewhere smaller, you know, better for families."

There was nothing funny about the irony, and Evan knew from personal experience that the memory of that decision would sneak up on her in her most vulnerable moments.

"Where was your husband employed?"

"Seminole Insurance," Karen answered.

Evan knew it; they had offices all over Florida. "Can you tell me his supervisor or manager's name?"

"Um…Carl," she answered. Her eyes darted around the wall behind him like someone might have scribbled the name there. "Carl Nelson."

"How did your husband like it there?"

She nodded. "He liked it. I mean, he's worked for Seminole since before we got married. Um, he started there in 2002, a couple of years after he graduated from FSU." She brushed a lock of hair behind her ear, her hand trembling. "He's won all kinds of awards and things, you know, for sales and customer retention, that kind of thing."

Evan nodded as he wrote, then looked back up at her. "Later today, after you've had some time with your pastor and your mother, I'd really appreciate you writing down the names of his friends and family, coworkers, former coworkers, whoever you can think of. With their numbers, if you have them."

"Okay." She swallowed hard and nodded. "I can do that."

"We have his phone, we'll need to keep it for just a bit, but your list could help us know who his contacts are without having to disturb all of them."

"Okay," she said distractedly.

"But at the moment, you can't think of anyone he's had any trouble with recently?"

"No, not at all. Not even in the past," she answered. "There—we had a neighbor back in Tallahassee that couldn't stand Jake because Jake called the police about his dog, but his dog—it was a Rottweiler—the dog was always running loose and coming in the yard. Jake was worried about the girls, you know?"

Evan nodded. "That's probably not relevant, but if you can add the neighbor to that list, I'd appreciate it." He tapped his pen against the notepad for a moment. "What about your husband's family? Are they close?"

She shook her head. "His parents are both gone. Cancer. He has a brother, Lance, who's in the Army in Germany." She swallowed. "I'll need to call him."

"Okay, Karen," Evan said. "Has there been anything unusual happening in the last few weeks?"

"Like what?"

Evan shrugged. "Jake get into it with anybody in traffic? Have you had any prowlers, anyone around the house that you don't know?"

She only had to think for a moment. "No, nothing like that."

"Please don't be offended, but has Jake ever been in trouble with the law?"

"Oh, Lord no." She almost smiled. "You don't understand. He was a missionary kid, one of the rare missionary kids that never went through some kind of rebellious period. Because of the way he grew up, moving from Peru to Panama to the DR, he was always really anxious to put down roots, to stay in one place for a long time, or forever."

She looked over at a silver-framed photograph on the end table. Karen and her husband, much younger, both of them wearing flowered shirts, big smiles, and painful-looking sunburns. She nodded at it. "We were only twenty-five when we got married. We didn't have any money, so we took one of those cheap four-day cruises to the Bahamas." She swallowed and flicked a tear away from her eye. "We felt so fancy and grown-up."

She looked back at Evan. "He worked really hard for us, for me and the kids." Her eyes pooled suddenly. "It's really important that you understand what a good guy he was."

Evan couldn't wait to leave.

"It seems like he was a very good man, Karen," he said. "I promise you that we'll remember that."

Several minutes later, Evan opened the door for Karen's pastor, a man of about thirty, wearing faded jeans and a bright white polo shirt. He was completely focused on Karen, and Evan had to respect the man's way with her. His compassion and warmth seemed genuine without being cloying. Evan didn't hear a single platitude in the few minutes he observed them.

Karen asked the pastor to help her tell her kids, and he agreed. Evan collected Goff, who was standing in the open sliding glass door in the kitchen, watching the Bellamy girls kick a ball back and forth. Evan slid his card and a pamphlet on victim support onto the coffee table, picked up Bellamy's license, and heard the pastor begin to pray as he and Goff quietly shut the front door behind them.

The two men didn't speak until Evan had backed out of the driveway, then Goff looked over at Evan. "What'd you learn from the wife?"

"They've only been here since Thanksgiving. Bellamy worked for Seminole Insurance, got a transfer here. Karen said he'd settled in nicely, no problems. She doesn't think they've been in town long enough to make any enemies."

"Maybe the enemies followed from their previous town," Goff mused. "Or it was mistaken identity."

"Maybe. He runs regularly, same route all the time. Two evenings a week that change, but every Saturday morning about the same time."

"Huh."

"Off the bat, he doesn't sound like a target for anger, but it sure looks like someone targeted him, specifically," Evan said.

"If so," Goff said, "he made an easy target. That bridge is a perfect funnel point, and those trees would make a pretty good blind."

"Yeah," Evan answered. They got to a stop sign and he rolled down his window, lit a much-needed cigarette.

"Sometimes I wish I smoked," Goff said quietly to the windshield.

"Sometimes I'm glad I do," Evan replied.

FIVE

IT ONLY TOOK A FEW minutes to get back to the crime scene, but when Evan turned onto Forest Park Avenue, it had already become congested with news vans and the cars belonging to print reporters. Rather than parking on either side of the street, half the news vans were blocking the road just outside the barricade formed by two PD cruisers.

Evan sighed and put the Pilot in park.

"Pretty easy to pick 'em off from here," Goff said.

"No, I'll go talk to them, then see if I can keep them out of our hair," Evan said, opening his door.

Evan's black Pilot didn't exactly stand out in the area, and he wasn't exactly dressed for work, either, so he was halfway to the cluster of reporters and cameramen before they started noticing him. Then they all rushed him at once, shouting out questions and pointing huge microphones his way. Evan held up his hands and looked each reporter in the eye until they'd all shut up.

"I'm not going to be answering any questions today, but—"

"But what can you tell us about the body in the park?" a blonde woman asked.

Evan stared at her. "That's a question. I will make a brief—very brief—statement, for now," he said. "The body of a male was found in the park early this morning. Cause of death has not yet been determined. The family has been notified, but we will not be releasing the man's name at this time."

"Can you at least tell us if this was a homicide?" a man with an unfortunate goatee asked.

"No. We're still processing the scene, and this investigation is only a few hours old," Evan said. "Once we have more useful information for you, we'll make another statement."

A red-haired woman took a step forward, poking a mic and a disdainful look in Evan's direction. He recognized her from one of the 5:30 broadcasts out of Panama City.

"*Acting* Sheriff Caldwell, you have a responsibility to the people of Gulf County and Port St. Joe," she said.

"This man and his family *are* the people of Gulf County and Port St. Joe," Evan answered. "You're from Bay County, aren't you?" Evan looked past her to the rest of the reporters, letting her know their repartee was done. "I'll let you know more as soon as I'm able, but I won't know more until I can get back to my job, so I'd appreciate it very much if those of you blocking the street would kindly move your vehicles. That's all for now."

A few people shot out questions or complaints, but Evan turned around and walked back to his SUV. He and Goff waited in silence until there was room for Evan to pull through. One of the patrolmen inched his cruiser out of the way, allowing Evan to pull back into the spot he'd left less than an hour earlier.

When he and Goff walked back to the crime scene, they found Crenshaw picking up evidence markers and Trigg cross-checking them with a list on her clipboard. She nodded at Evan and Goff as they went by, on their way back to the embankment.

Danny was crouched down next to the body of Jake Bellamy, but he looked to be packing up his things.

"What can you tell me, Danny?" Evan asked as he and Goff made their way to him.

"Oh, hey, Sheriff," Danny said brightly. "Yeah, so livor mortis had started already when I got here, most notably in the torso, feet, and hands, but the blood wasn't fixed yet. Once we turned him onto his back the blood moved to his back and buttocks. So, as you probably already know, he was on his stomach at time of death or immediately after."

"Okay," Evan said. "Based on liver temp compared to ambient temp, and the fact that rigor mortis is just now becoming evident in the eyelids, jaw, and neck, I'm tentatively calling TOD at somewhere between 6:30 and 7:00 am. Anyhoo," he said, rubbing his hands in either relish or a need to warm up, "Your cause of death is exsanguination due to multiple punctures to the upper right quadrant. I won't know how many perforations there are until I get him back home and tidied up a little because you have several overlapping wounds. Of course, I'll have a clearer picture once I've had a look-see inside, but I'm thinking there are at least five or six punctures that would have killed him."

All of this was said in the blink of an eye, and Evan was glad the kid finally took a breath, his bony chest caving with the effort. Evan glanced at Goff, who was looking at him.

"Feller's dead," Goff said, apparently thinking Evan needed translation.

"Oh yeah," Danny said, all wide-eyed innocence. "Essentially, for sure."

Evan nodded at Goff. "I caught that." He looked back at Danny. "There are quite a few defensive wounds on his hands."

"Oh, yeah. Looks like he fought pretty hard, the poor sucker," Danny said. "He didn't die easily."

"Any thoughts on weapon?" Evan asked.

Danny zipped his duffel and stood. "Just that we're looking at a thin blade. I won't know length or any blade curvature until I get in there. One oddity, for me, is that there aren't any slash marks to the torso. A few on the hands, right, but none to the body."

"Why's that weird?" Goff asked.

"Well, in my experience, okay not experience because this is my first death by stabbing, but in my studies, when you have this much violence, probably rage, right? When you have this much, and especially if the guy's fighting back, you'll see more slashes. You know, trying to get the job done and over with. But the guy doing the stabbing in this case, he only slashed at the hands and forearms then, we can suppose, moved in for, you know, stabbing."

"Well, I agree with you about the anger," Evan said. "Since the killer didn't even check Bellamy's runner's belt, we can assume he was targeted for something other than robbery."

All three of them looked at the body a moment, Danny with his hands on his hips, nodding down at the man like he'd just said something.

"You ready for the paramedics to come down here and help you bag him up?" Evan asked.

"Yeah, I'm ready to head back to the lab," Danny said. "I also have to pee."

Evan looked at Goff. "Can you get the paramedics?" he asked. "I'm gonna go see what's happening with the neighborhood canvass."

Goff nodded, and they both headed back up the embankment. Trigg was following Crenshaw back to the street.

"You done?" Evan called from behind her.

She stopped and waited a second for him to catch up. "Yeah, I've got everything we're gonna get."

"Anything besides the blood?"

They started walking again. "Not really. I pulled a couple of fibers from his jacket and a hair from the zipper pull. Brown, but not his. Not helpful unless the DNA belongs to someone in the system, but we'll see. Goofier things have happened."

"That's true," Evan said.

"I also got a few partial shoe prints where the grass was sparse by the trees, but who knows. Some are certainly the victim's. How'd the notification go?"

Evan stopped by Trigg's Jeep Liberty, watched as she opened the door and started putting her kit away. Crenshaw had already loaded most of the gear and evidence into the cargo area.

"It sucked," Evan answered. "Young wife, two little girls." He sighed. "They just moved here for a better, safer place to raise their kids."

"That does suck," Trigg said quietly, closing her door.

Cops had a tendency to crack jokes or see the dark humor in a violent death or a crime scene. It was almost necessary, as it created distance between them and the victims; a distance that helped them do their jobs. But, once a cop met the victim's dog, once they smelled the pot roast that the victim wouldn't make it home to eat or saw the family pictures on the back of the piano,

detachment became more difficult. In Evan's experience, it was the personal details, the loved ones, that
drove some cops to divorce, pills, and alcohol. The line
between professional detachment and personal burden
was a tough one to walk.

"You have anything in line ahead of this one?" Evan
asked.

"Nope. Just some prints and DNA from that robbery
in White City," she said. "Moving that back."

"Good. I'm gonna go see if anything useful has turned
up in the canvass," he said.

"A neighbor who answers the door holding a bloody
knife would be nice," Paula said.

"Wouldn't it?" Evan walked over to where Goff and a
group of several deputies and patrolmen were clustered.
He recognized a few of them as being officers he'd sent
out on the first canvass.

"Anybody get anything worthwhile, a witness, anything?" he asked.

"Not really," Goff answered. "One lady over on Marvin,
right across from the park, said her dog went nuts
around 6:30, but she just yelled at him to shut up, so she
doesn't know if it meant anything. Another guy," Goff
looked down at his notes, "name of Brewster, lives on
20th. He says he's always up by five. He went out to his
car to get something around twenty after six and said
a guy jogged by, guy he's seen jogging before. Descrip-

tion he gave sounds like our vic, but he said he didn't see anybody else."

Evan sighed. "How many people didn't answer their doors?"

"Maybe twenty-percent for me," one patrolman said.

"Yeah, about that," Crenshaw added.

"Okay, hand your streets over to some fresh blood, have them check every resident that hasn't been spoken to yet," Evan said. "Some were asleep, some were already out buying blankets and mittens, and so on. I want you to keep passing addresses down until everyone has either been spoken to or confirmed to be dead or up north."

· ● ✳ ● ·

The Gulf County Sheriff's Office was located on a nondescript, almost treeless stretch of Cecil G. Costin, Sr. Boulevard, which became Hwy 71 a few blocks further on. Hwy 71 was mainly used by locals and tourists traveling to and from points east and north.

The Sheriff's Office was set quite a way off the road, sandwiched between the library and the county courthouse. All three buildings were of characterless architecture and painted in various shades of what Evan thought of as Florida government desert camo. Of the three buildings, the SO was the smallest and had the least parking.

Evan pulled into his usual spot. He and Goff said their hellos or returned nods as they made their way to Evan's office in the back. Just outside his office, serving as both a barrier and an anteroom, was the kingdom of Vi Hartigan. As he made his way down the hall, he could see Vi stationed at her desk, tapping away on her computer.

Vi was a slim, deeply tanned woman somewhere in her sixties, with sparse, close-cropped hair that looked like the down of some exotic red bird. The birdlike appearance was somewhat enhanced by her beaklike nose. Perched at its tip was a pair of teal bifocals on a beaded chain. The glasses matched her dramatic dreamcatcher earrings.

When Evan and Goff walked through the open doorway to her office, she frowned up at them and removed her glasses, letting them fall against a blouse covered in palm trees.

"Mr. Caldwell," she intoned in a voice that always reminded him of Walter Cronkite. "Why are you here?"

"You called me, Vi."

"I relayed a request for you to respond to the scene, as you should given the severity," she replied. "I did not intend for you to come back to the office."

"Why wouldn't I?"

"Perhaps because you've worked every day for the last thirty-two days."

"I think your math is wrong," Evan said.

"Aw, geez," he heard Goff mutter behind him.

"Is that so?" Vi asked, pulling a desk calendar toward her. She dropped her glasses back onto the tip of her

DAWN LEE MCKENNA & AXEL BLACKWELL

nose and read, flipping pages with more violence than was probably needed. "Work. Work. Work. Oh, you're right." She looked up at him. "I apologize. You took an hour off to get your hair cut three weeks ago, on the 5th."

"You're here," Evan responded.

"I'm *scheduled* to be here every other Saturday, as you know."

"I appreciate your concern, Vi, but we have a homicide on our hands," Evan said. "We need to maximize our time in the next few days, and there are things I need to get done. Now."

"I see." She peered at him over her glasses, and Evan thought he felt Goff move back just a hair. "Between us, Sgt. Goff and I have over fifty years' experience in this department. Is there something on your agenda so complex that it precludes delegation to one of us?"

"Background checks and phone calls to the contacts the victim's wife gave me."

"Oh, my. That is intricate," Vi replied flatly.

Goff coughed softly behind Evan. "Reckon he was just about to hand that off to me, Vi," he said.

Evan scratched at his scar for a moment. "I thought maybe Goff could make the phone calls and you could pull the background checks," he lied.

"Excellent," she replied, looking back at her monitor. "Please get me the names as soon as possible. I need to get home in time to make my no-bake cookies for Scrabble club tonight."

"How long can it take to not bake cookies?" Evan asked, against his better judgment.

Vi's forehead compressed like an accordion as she glared over her bifocals at him.

"Thank you, Vi," Evan said, and walked to his door and opened it.

Goff followed Evan in, then quietly shut the door behind him. "I don't know why you're so compelled to push with that woman," he said.

Evan smiled. "I'm not scared of Vi."

"Nobody is until they are," Goff replied. "You know she's the Jacker Whacker, right?"

Evan sat at his desk. "The what?"

Goff deposited his bony frame in the vinyl chair in front of Evan's desk. "Few years back, feller tried to snatch her keys from her over at the Dollar General, while she was putting her bags in the trunk. Almost dislocated her shoulder. She beat the crap out of him with a jar of bread-and-butter pickles, then backed over his foot when she was pulling out. Called it in herself at the red light."

"No kidding."

"Nope. It was all on the parking lot cameras. We played it at her birthday party last year."

"Your cautionary tale is noted," Evan said, pulling out his black notepad. "Okay, this is the handful of contacts that Karen Bellamy was able to give me. She has phone numbers for most. We also need to pull contacts from Bellamy's phone. You handle the calls. Split them up

DAWN LEE MCKENNA & AXEL BLACKWELL

with someone on duty if you want to. We want to know when these people last saw or spoke to Bellamy, if they knew of anyone he had problems with, if he'd discussed anything weird or upsetting or just out of the ordinary. I know you know what we're after; I'm running over it as much for myself as for you."

"Gotcha," Goff said.

"Here, do me a favor, have Vi make a couple copies of this, will you?"

Goff took the notebook and walked back out to Vi's area, shutting the door behind him.

Evan sat back in his leather chair and ran a hand over his face. He was, according to the foster care system, half Cuban by way of his teenaged mother, but he hadn't been out in the sun much lately. Though Cubans weren't necessarily naturally dark, he knew he was looking a little pallid. When he'd gotten up this morning after a night of intermittent sleep, he'd thought about taking the boat out today. Then everything got screwed up, Jake Bellamy got dead, and Evan knew for a fact that he'd been glad to spend his day thinking about someone's life other than his own.

Goff came back into the office, and when he made to close the door, Evan waved at him.

"Leave it, it's stuffy in here with this heat on," he said.

Goff left the door open and came back to the desk, slid the notebook back across. He held a copy of the contacts list.

"Thank you," Evan said.

He was about to say something else when the intercom buzzed. He pressed down on the button. "Yes, Vi."

"This is Vi," she said in stereo. He could hear her through the open door. "I have my list."

"Okay," Evan said.

"You're free to go."

· ● ✳ ● ·

An hour later, Evan walked past the Dockside Grill, an indoor/outdoor restaurant located at the front of the Port St. Joe Marina. It being a Saturday afternoon, the place was hopping. Popular with local as well as visiting boaters, the Dockside did a good business. It had good fresh seafood and burgers, a friendly staff, and a tiki-tropical feel to the outdoor dining decks. Speakers strewn around the place played a combination of 70s pop and reggae, but not so loud that Evan hated them for it.

Evan walked down the wide steps that led from a firepit/conversation area down to the dock, two grocery bags in each hand. Piggly-Wiggly was at the entrance to the marina, and he'd gone back to finish his grocery shopping on the way home.

He turned left and headed around the fish cleaning station and along Pier A, nodding at a few people who were doing some of the endless housekeeping familiar to all boat owners. Other folks lounged on deck chairs, sipping bottled beer or reading paperback books borrowed from the marina library.

Evan's houseboat was located at the end of the pier. He'd been lucky to snag the T-head spot with 50amp service. It was easy to dock his 50-foot boat and to get underway, and he was allowed to tie his much smaller Sea Fox up behind his stern as long as no one needed the space. He had a great view from his starboard side of the channel and St. Joseph Bay, separated from the Gulf by a thin spit of land called the St. Joseph Peninsula, which belonged to the St. Joseph Bay Aquatic Preserve.

Evan's home was a 1986 Chris-Craft Corinthian that Evan had managed to get for a song when he'd moved to Port St. Joe. The owner had been meticulous in his care of the motor yacht, and it was worth a lot more, but the guy had been involved in a nasty divorce and needed to unload it fast. Even after selling his house in Cocoa Beach, medical bills left very little for living expenses. Slip rent on the boat was less than a decent one-bedroom condo, and Evan was grateful for it.

It had a spacious aft deck, with room for a grill, a rattan dining set, and a few chairs. The aft deck had been the deciding factor for Evan. He slipped out of his deck shoes and picked them up, then stepped onto the deck. He stowed the shoes in a cubby next to the glass door, then went inside.

The taupe carpet in the salon and staterooms was one of the few things Evan didn't like about the boat. It was clean enough to look new, but Evan preferred wood, especially with a cat that tended to yak and hack. Evan had never had a cat before, or any other pet for that matter, and he had no idea if this was normal behavior, but he took it personally anyway.

There was no sign of Plutes as Evan crossed the salon and took the three steps down to the galley, but once there, he found the huge, black cat sitting on top of the refrigerator. His wife had brought the thing home about two weeks before her accident. It was only after she'd been hurt that he'd learned the cat had actually belonged to his wife's boyfriend. It was the boyfriend that had shared that information with him. Even if Evan had been a cat person, which he was not, this would have worked against their chances of a relationship.

Evan put the grocery bags on the dinette booth, then unclipped his badge, removed his service weapon from its holster, and put them down as well. As he started unpacking the bags, he saw that the salt shaker lay on its side on the small gas stove, salt spread around it like arterial blood. A few days earlier, Evan had found the ruined body of an African violet on the couch. A trail of black dirt led back to the shelf under the window and the remains of a little clay pot. Evan was becoming used to these types of commentary.

"You should know that I've spent a good part of my day pondering the cat food situation," Evan said as he put away a couple of ripe tomatoes. Plutes regarded him through narrowed eyes, one ear flattening backward. "Although, having now read the labels on all the crap I've been buying you, I can almost understand your issues."

Evan placed a head of lettuce in the fridge and took out a pint carton of coconut water. He popped the tab, took a swallow, then put it down on the counter. He pulled two Styrofoam trays of fish out of the last bag.

"We're grilling some fish tonight," Evan said. "I'm having this gorgeous grouper, with a little tarragon and lime. You're having tilapia because you can't read."

He stuffed the grocery bags into the little plastic container hanging by the utility cupboard, then pulled out his Dustbuster, and clicked it on.

"If you'd like some salt for your fish, you can come lick it off of the stove, because we are now out of salt," he said as he vacuumed the grains from the stove.

He looked up at Plutes, then pointed the Dustbuster at him. The cat jumped from the fridge to the counter and from there over to the dinette table. Evan turned off the Dustbuster and put it away. When he turned back around, Plutes was doing his impression of Don Knotts choking on a chicken bone.

"Not on the—get down!" he snapped. He went to reach for Plutes just as the cat opened his mouth and something like a furry, black, baby anaconda slid out onto Evan's badge. Evan sighed, and the cat peered down at his product like he was Inspector #12, then jumped down from the table and trotted up the steps to the salon.

Evan had read somewhere that slugs vomited up their young. He looked at the thing on his badge, which was beginning to sweat, and could see why slugs had never really taken off as house pets.

"Dinner will be ready in thirty minutes," Evan called out. "Go wash your feet."

SIX

IT HAD INDEED GOTTEN as low as twenty during the night, and each time Evan woke up, he had pulled the covers a little higher, burrowing in a pocket of warmth that should have brought a more peaceful sleep. He'd finally gotten up at just after six and turned off the phone alarm that he rarely needed.

After pulling on some sweats and a heavy hoodie, he brushed his teeth and went up to the galley. He cranked up the espresso machine, popped his milk into the microwave, and then put some leftover fish in the cat's stainless-steel bowl. Then Evan carried his *café con leche* out to the aft deck, leaving the glass door open for Plutes. This was one of the rare times that Evan didn't have all of the windows open, and the litter box was out on the deck. Unless the cat learned to use the head, he was going to have to poop outside.

Evan sipped his coffee, his breath puffing outward and becoming one with the steam from his cup. The sky was just starting to lighten, and though it was cool, there wasn't a cloud in the sky. The bay was glassy. It would be a great day to go out, though Evan preferred a nice chop.

He picked up his cigarettes and lighter from the small glass table, lit a cigarette, and enjoyed the first, almost crushing, lungful of the day. He wondered, not for the first time, why the first drag of the day was the best, despite the fact that it was almost painful. He'd quit for almost seven years. Almost a year ago, he'd walked out of the emergency room in Cape Canaveral, walked past the ambulance that had transported his wife, and bummed a smoke off of a guy with a cigarette in one hand and his IV pole in another.

Evan had felt a rush of guilt as he bent for a light, quickly followed by a sweeping calm as he breathed in his first hit of nicotine in years. The guilt had returned later that day as he bought his own pack of Marlboros, and he had vowed to quit again as soon as his wife was better.

Evan watched Plutes step into his cat box, as gingerly as a twenty-pound cat could, and turn around several times before choosing the right square centimeter of litter box real estate on which to deposit his morning pee. Evan blew smoke rings as he watched the cat check to make sure he had, in fact, urinated, and then step out of the box, shaking grit from his feet onto the deck.

"That's okay, I'll get that," Evan said quietly, as the cat jumped up onto one of the built-in lockers. "You putz."

He turned to crush out his cigarette in the ashtray and saw The Muffin Girl coming down the dock, a canvas tote in each hand. He leaned on the rail and watched her come.

Although he now knew her to be Sarah, for the first two months he'd lived there he'd thought of her as The Muffin Girl because every Sunday morning she delivered the paper and a home-baked muffin, compliments of the marina.

She was a tiny little thing, about five-two and less than a hundred pounds. She reminded him of some kind of punk fairy, with her spiky, short black hair and her various piercings. Normally clad in cutoffs and old tee shirts, she looked particularly small today, in baggy black sweatpants and a bright pink Victoria's Secret hoodie. Although her father was an infamous meth cooker and every male in her family had done time, she was a nice kid. At seventeen, she was on her own, and did odd jobs around the marina, like hosing down the docks, delivering papers, and stocking shelves in the small marina store. In exchange, aside from minimum wage, she lived rent-free on a small sailboat and got three meals a day at the Dockside Grill. Evan doubted that she ate much.

"Hey," she said as she approached, in a high, breathy voice that always surprised him.

"Hey," he said back.

"Hey, Plutes," she said to the cat, who had jumped down to the dive platform at the sound of her voice.

"Are you keeping warm over there?"

"Yeah, sure," she said. "I've got a new space heater." She caught his look. "Don't worry, it's one of those infrared ones. It's cool."

"You want to sit?"

She looked down at her high-top sneakers. "I would, but it would be a pain to take these off."

"It's okay," he told her. He wondered why it was okay when it never was with anyone else.

Evan watched her as she came aboard, and up the steps to the aft deck. She flopped down in one of the rattan chairs, dropping the totes on the deck. Plutes jumped down and went to her, winding himself around her ankles. Evan wanted to throw up. The cat never so much as sat next to him, much less twirled around his legs.

Sarah leaned over and heaved the cat up onto her lap. "Don't you wonder why he never talks?" she asked.

"No. He's a cat. He can't speak."

She tossed him a look, but it was tempered with a little grin. "No, I mean he never meows or anything." She blinked as Plutes dragged his tail across her face.

Evan had noticed, but he'd figured the cat just didn't have anything to say to him.

"Maybe you should take him to the vet," Sarah said, spitting a fluff of black hair from her lower lip.

"I took him last month. For his shots," Evan said. "The vet didn't say anything about it."

"Did you ask him?"

"No," Evan answered, a little defensively.

"Tell him next time," she said.

"Okay, Mom." He drained his coffee. "You want some coffee?"

"No, thanks," she said. "I only drink tea."

"I don't have any."

"That's okay, I already had some." Plutes jumped down and padded over to the rail where he settled to the deck and watched her. Sarah pulled a blueberry muffin wrapped in plastic out of her tote. "Here."

He took it, though he seldom ate the muffins. "Thank you."

He watched her reach into the other bag. He was her last stop, and the only paper left was his. It was wrapped in a rubber band. Even on Sundays, the paper was thin.

He took the paper from her, gave her half a smile as he pulled the rubber band off. "Let's see what we have today," he said, as she watched him expectantly. He unrolled the paper. Inside was a small piece of paper, a handwritten note on a marina notepad.

"Have you ever accidentally given this to the wrong person?" he asked. He already knew he was the only one who got the additional insert.

"Nope. I always put a red rubber band on yours," she said.

"Ah." He unfurled the note and read it out loud. "Consider the blameless, observe the upright, a future awaits those who seek peace. Psalm 37:37." He looked over at her and gave her what he hoped was a grateful smile. "Thank you."

"It made me think of you, 'cause you need some peace."

"Do I?" he asked her. It was a silly question. Even he knew he needed some kind of respite. He knew he was just being coy.

"Don't you?" she asked.

Evan nodded at her as he folded the note and tucked it into his pocket.

"I know you probably throw those away, but I just feel like you need a good word here and there," she said, shrugging. "I heard about that guy that got stabbed in the park," she said. "That sucks."

Evan didn't bother asking how she heard; he'd seen the front page. Somebody always talked to the press. "Yeah, it does. He had a wife and two little girls."

Sarah sighed, a large sigh for such a tiny body. "You know how the Bible says God is so patient?" He gave a noncommittal nod. "You know how I know it's true? 'Cause if I was God, this whole show would have been over a long time ago. I know you've seen all kinds of terrible stuff. I can't imagine what it's like for Him to see all of it. I'd be done," she added with a snap of her fingers.

Evan nodded at her. He'd never thought about it. She reached over and gave Plutes a quick rub, then stood and brushed at the fur that coated her sweats, to no effect at all.

"I gotta go. One of the prep cooks called out, so I gotta go slice tomatoes and stuff." She picked up her empty totes. "You off today?"

Evan shrugged one shoulder; he didn't really know the answer to that question.

"You gonna go see your wife?"

"Yeah," he answered.

She nodded as she walked past him and hopped to the dock. "I pray for her all the time."

Evan swallowed hard. "What do you pray?"

He didn't know Sarah well, but one of the things he liked about her was that she was completely frank, and unapologetic about it. Artifice wasn't natural for her, and he watched her struggle with it now, biting the corner of her lip.

"That you'll both have healing," she said. "I'll see you around."

He nodded a goodbye and watched her a moment as she walked back up the dock. Plutes had nothing left on the aft deck to interest him, and he walked inside, tail standing straight up, like a burnt but intact mast.

Evan followed him inside, leaving the glass door propped open. He walked over to a built-in teak cabinet, opened the wooden box that sat on top, and put the folded notepaper inside with the others.

· ● ✳ ● ·

Sunset Bay was located on the eastern edge of town, nestled between a park and a tennis club. A long, winding driveway curled between neatly trimmed lawns and flowerbeds that were a riot of colors at any time of the year. In the middle of a parklike setting, not unlike that of the Buck Griffin crime scene, was a small man-made lake. In the middle of that, a fountain sent a circular spray of water that arched back downward and hit the water with a sound like gentle rain.

There were several black iron benches positioned around the lake, but no one sat on them. It was a cool morning, and Evan rarely saw anyone sitting by the water.

Evan parked in front of the main building, a two-story, vaguely Mediterranean structure that could have been a country club or a decent hotel. On either side of it were neatly organized clusters of one-story buildings that contained six apartments each, as well as a small nurse's station to serve them. They were costly, but the care and attention at Sunset Bay were costly, too, and cut no corners. The apartments were a pleasant compromise for seniors who were well enough to live on their own, but well off enough to not have to.

Evan crossed the elegant lobby of the main building, past deep red clusters of seating and original oils of the Florida Panhandle, his heels clicking solidly on the herringbone floor. He nodded at the security guard who no longer asked him to check in, then took the elevator up one floor.

He emerged into a scene far different from the neatly decorated apartments in the other buildings. This environment was just as thoughtfully decorated, but clearly a hospital floor. He said hello back to a young blonde nurse who passed him in the hallway, then pushed open the door to Room 209.

Pale yellow shades were drawn against the powerful, late morning sun, casting the room in a golden light. The cherry dresser against one wall glittered in the diffused sunshine, and the seascape hanging above it seemed to try to bring the outdoors in, even as the shades kept the outdoors out.

There was a small cherry table next to an upholstered chair. The mauve velvet upholstery matched the mauve coverlet on the hospital bed. Evan walked to it, stood with his hands on the rail.

Hannah seemed paler than she had just a day ago, her almost perfect skin a jarring contrast to her dark brown hair, cut in a shaggy pixie. On the little end table, a silver-framed photograph of the two of them on a cruise showed her wearing the same hairstyle, though she'd grown it out quite a bit before her accident. He appreciated the effort to give her a haircut she might like.

Despite the fact that she'd lost at least twenty pounds from her tall, already slim frame, despite the gray shadows beneath her eyes and the lack of color to her lips, she was still a beautiful woman. At thirty-six, she had just started developing little laugh lines at the corner of her mouth, small furrows between her eyes, but they were gone now.

Her lips weren't as chapped as they had been when she'd had the ventilator. They'd given her a tracheotomy not long ago, in the interest of minimizing damage to her throat, and the tube that ran to it was covered by a small square of white dressing. He appreciated that, too.

He walked around the bed, lifted the paper shade a bit for his own mental health, and sat down in the chair, his black suit trousers making a quiet swish as he put his right foot on his left knee. He noticed his shoes needed a good buffing, but there was an identical pair in his closet that was ready to go.

He looked up at the face of his wife of five short years. "So, I've put your cat on a clean food diet," he said conversationally. "Have you ever read the ingredients list on cat food? It's ridiculous to pay that much for garbage, and he throws it all up, anyway. But, clearly, I haven't tossed him overboard, as I'm sure you would have expected."

Evan already wanted a cigarette, although the need was probably just to get outside, away. It disappointed him.

"Caught a new case. A homicide," he said after a moment of silence that would have been awkward with anyone else. "The guy had a wife waiting at home, two little girls. Next of kin visits don't get any easier."

In fact, Evan thought they'd gotten harder since he'd had one of his own. He'd just finished testifying on one of his cases when he'd gotten the call to go to the hospital. He remembered his head spinning, his feet and fingers becoming tingly and then numb as he'd listened to the ER doctor talking. Swelling of the brain, hematomas, aneurysms, clots. It had gotten worse later that night when she'd gone from plain unconsciousness to coma. All because she'd stepped at the wrong moment, foot poised over the water, someone's wake causing the boat to rock, and she'd fallen. Hit her head precisely just so on the edge of the dock.

Her boyfriend, Shayne, was a complete surprise, sitting at one end of the waiting area while Evan sat at the other. He still visited once a month or so, but never when Evan was present. Her mom, who lived across the state, had stopped coming. It was just too hard, and she had done her mourning.

Evan shook himself out of his own head and quietly told Hannah about the cleaning he needed to do on the brightwork, as soon as it warmed up again. That he'd found a new favorite hot sauce, a locally-made brand called Ed's Red. How funny it was that sleeping with her had been such an adjustment, but now he found it difficult to sleep alone. He told her about the Carjacker Whacker and the fish he'd prepared for him and Plutes the night before, and how cold it had been when he'd gone out to the aft deck for his ritual golden milk before bed.

He didn't mention that his last cigarette of the night was part of the ritual, although, if asked, he wouldn't have been able to explain why. Not with any real conviction.

After another thirty minutes of searching for new things to say, Evan stood, bent over the bed rail to kiss Hannah's cool, dry forehead, and got out of there before her doctor could come by to gently remind him that decisions needed to be made.

SEVEN

BY THE TIME EVAN got back to town, it was midafternoon. Most of the after-church lunch rush was winding down, but when he pulled into the Dockside Grill, it was still packed. When he walked to the back, he saw that there was some kind of party going on. Through the windows, he could see every table occupied, nearly every inch of floor space crowded. Old couples in church clothes tottered back and forth between tables, nearly tripping over young children. Teenagers huddled in conspiratorial clusters in the booths, whispering and giggling. Proud parents with weary but resplendent smiles bounced wriggly little bundles. Evan guessed it must be a family reunion, or maybe an anniversary.

He was starving but lost all touch with that sensation. The crowd wasn't what killed his appetite. A deeper hunger had replaced it. He felt like he was looking into a snow globe, like he was seeing the promise of a perfect world where every child had two parents, where life is long, and tears are few, where every old man was a grandfather and there were no widows. Or orphans. Where there was no beautiful young wife shriveling in a hospital bed because her husband wasn't what she needed him to be.

Anything can look ideal from outside the glass; Evan knew this. Snow globes and Thomas Kinkade paintings only look perfect because they are fake. But poor sleep combined with his job and his daily visits to Hannah were conspiring to make him feel morose. He had a tendency to let himself slide into a little depression, but he was rarely maudlin or fatalistic. He needed to start sleeping again.

He noticed Benny behind the bar, flipping glassware and flashing his infectious smile. A slim black man with long, throwback sideburns, the barman was halfway through his junior year, going for his Masters in elementary education. With his charisma and spirit, he would make a great teacher. The kid was Port St. Joe born and bred, and Evan usually enjoyed his stories about the area and his corny jokes; they were usually just what he needed after a long day.

Dockside was just too crowded today, too boisterous and noisy. He turned around and walked back to his Pilot before Benny saw him, and drove back out to Monument. He hung a right, then crossed the busy main drag to pull into Krazyfish.

The place looked like a beachside bar that someone had accidentally left on Monument Avenue, with its bright turquoise exterior, multicolored tables and chairs, and a patio for eating outside. After parking, he looked up at the restaurant windows. Inside, Jordan Scruggs was waiting tables. Evan groaned.

He had heard good things about Krazyfish, but he'd never actually eaten there. Jordan was one of the reasons why. He had promised her dying father that he would keep an eye on her and her daughter, Avery. The guy, Scruggs, had built up quite a reputation and criminal record for himself but had decided, on the brink of extinction, that he should probably try to do something good. He'd been a help in the investigation of Sheriff Hutchens' death, and Evan hadn't had the heart to decline when he asked Evan to keep an eye on Jordan and her baby.

This put him in the middle of an ongoing custody dispute, which was less than heartwarming. More importantly, Jordan also tended to be a bit more expressive than Evan was comfortable with. She was a very pretty girl, but she was only in her early twenties, and Evan had no interest at all, wouldn't have even if he was single. She'd misconstrued his willingness to keep his promise to her father, tried to install Evan as her new go-to guy for anything from emotional support to babysitting. He had put a stop to that, with extreme prejudice, but still felt like he had to have his personal shields at maximum whenever she was within touching distance.

He didn't have the emotional energy for her just then, so, when he spotted her tending her tables and flipping her ponytail like she was taming lions with it, he dialed the number on the wooden sign and called in his order rather than go inside. Shrimp tacos with jalapeno bacon marmalade sounded interesting enough.

He scanned through stations on the radio for a few minutes while waiting, then shut it off and popped open his laptop. The Jake Bellamy file, what little there was of it, was open. He had memorized the names Jake's widow had provided, local relatives, friends, coworkers. He had reviewed the photographs too often already, to the point that he had been somewhat desensitized to the violence they portrayed. This time, as he flipped through the images, he used a program that automatically inverted them, causing each to be less familiar to his eye. He hoped the difference in angle might lead to some new detail he had missed that may have been lost due to his familiarity with the photos.

He studied each shot, trying to put himself back at the scene, conjuring the sounds, the smells, the texture of the air. Nothing popped in the first dozen photos. He'd been through them twice more when there was a rap on his window. He turned to see Jordan leaning over to look in at him, a Styrofoam box in her hand.

Evan hit the button to lower the glass. "Hi, Jordan," he said. "I could've come in to get that."

"Oh, don't be silly," she said, leaning further into his car, "I needed an excuse to step out…Oh sick, is that that guy who got stabbed in the park?"

He quickly shut his laptop.

She stared at him for a moment then straightened a bit. "Well, I guess it ain't really my business, anyway, huh?"

"How much for the tacos?" Evan asked.

"Oh," she looked surprised. "It's on the house, Evan."

"No, Jordan. It's not on the house," he said with mock patience. "We're not allowed to accept gifts based on our law enforcement status."

"Well, my boss says I can't charge you for it." She looked at him with a hint of a pout and eyes that seemed to ask *how ever can we resolve this dilemma?* "You don't want me to get fired, do you?"

"No, I just want to eat my lunch," Evan said. He pulled a twenty out of his wallet and pressed it into her hand. "Here, take this. Call it a tip."

"Awww!" She drew it out like a ten-year-old seeing a newborn puppy. "You're such a good guy. She practically dove through his open window to hug him.

"Jordan!" he barked, nearly dropping his lunch.

"I'm sorry," she said, withdrawing, but smiling all the same. "It's just, you're so great…and, you really looked like you needed a hug, is all."

Evan tried for a kind smile but shook his head. "I'm sure I do."

DAWN LEE MCKENNA & AXEL BLACKWELL

She threw him an enigmatic smile, stepping away from his window. "I put some key lime in there for you."

Evan looked at the Styrofoam box. "Thanks. You staying out of trouble?"

"I don't have time for trouble, between work and my baby girl," she said. "I'm being good."

"Good. I've got to go," Evan said. He pushed the window up button. "Goodbye, Jordan," he said before it closed all the way.

"Goodbye, Evan!" she called, waving and giggling as he pulled out of the lot.

"We put the crazy in Krazyfish," he muttered, shaking his head. But the tacos smelled delicious, kicking his appetite back into gear. And Jordan, for all her lack of discretion, immaturity, and general boundary issues, had managed to take the edge off the irritating emptiness that had plagued his day.

From the parking lot, a right would take him home to the marina and his boat, a left would take him to the Sheriff's Office. Evan decided that on a Sunday afternoon, his best chance at solitude would be behind his closed office door. With no thought beyond that, he hooked a left.

Only a few other cars sat in the SO parking lot. In the lobby, Tosh Bradley slouched behind the front desk, arms folded, legs crossed. Evan understood, at first glance, that the kid's dark glasses served only one purpose, they hid his eyes, so no one would know he was asleep. It might have been a more effective ploy if he wasn't snoring.

His iPhone was propped sideways with its back against the telephone, live streaming college football. Evan thought it sounded like an exciting game, based on the announcer's voice, but apparently not quite exciting enough to keep Tosh awake.

Tosh had been employed by the SO as a mechanic/handyman for the past two years before being selected to attend the Law Enforcement Academy. Two weeks into his training, he had broken his wrist in a Defensive Tactics class and had to drop out. They'd let him take a second crack at it in a few months once his wrist had healed, but in the meantime, he was out of luck –- the mechanic job had been filled shortly after he vacated it.

Evan had agreed to keep him on as Mission Support, partly to tide him over, and partly to mitigate some of the distrust and unease that had resulted from Evan's sudden promotion and subsequent trashing of the former boss's formerly beloved reputation. Mission Support was a fancy title that meant Tosh got all the jobs nobody else wanted and that didn't require a badge and gun. That included front desk duty on Sunday afternoons.

Evan managed to make it past the front desk without waking its occupant. He could hear a two-finger typist punching out a report somewhere in the bullpen but didn't look in to see who it was. He walked straight to his office, his steps silent on the beige industrial carpet, past Vi's empty desk, and closed his office door behind him.

When this office had belonged to Sheriff Hutchens, the walls had been crowded with framed certificates, diplomas, community posters featuring the formerly popular Sheriff Hutchens, and, of course, several large photographs of Hutch shaking hands with various politicians, business leaders, star athletes, and one movie star. These had been collected by a representative of the family shortly after his case had been closed.

Evan did not have much in the way of wall décor, and not much interest in getting any. He had ordered a custom leather desk chair, which had arrived a few days back. It was a duplicate of the one he had used back in Brevard County and its familiarity relaxed him. His only other attempt at personalizing the office, at least so far, was a three-by-six corkboard he had intended to use for organizing leads, tips, persons of interest, and suspects when working larger cases. Until yesterday, there hadn't been any large cases on the books, so initially, he had simply tacked up wanted posters – now known as BOLOs or Be On the Look Out's – just so that the board wouldn't seem useless.

As Evan sat down and opened his lunch, he glanced up at the BOLO board and couldn't help smiling. Every deputy on staff grinned back at him, each with a wrong –- or ridiculously fake –- name pinned beneath their

photograph, and each wanted for some truly embar-
rassing or out of character crimes.

Within a week of taking over the office, and install-
ing the BOLO board, Evan had inadvertently called a
deputy by the wrong name during an all office meeting.
The following day, during morning muster, he again
called the same deputy by the wrong name, though it
was a different wrong name that time. When he arrived
at work the next morning, the pictures had been pinned
to his board. Each deputy's name had been written in
thick black marker on Post-it notes and pinned below
their photo. At the top of the board, the pranksters had
pinned the lower half of an old surveillance BOLO which
read, "If you can identify any of these subjects, please
call the Gulf County Sheriff's Office. You WILL remain
completely anonymous."

From the first day it appeared, the new BOLO board
had been a source of intense amusement to most of the
deputies and other office staff. The deputy's names were
always being scrambled or replaced with joke names.
Evan had never mentioned it, which made the responsible parties nuts, but he made no effort to stop it, nor
did he intend to. If he needed a corkboard to arrange
leads, he'd go buy a new one. This board was the first
of many jabs and counterstrikes he and his new team
would engage in over the next few months testing each
other's tolerance, each other's spirit, building a founda-

tion that someday might be able to support a structure as tenuous as trust.

Evan returned his attention to the desktop. It was clear except for a couple dozen properly organized, neatly stacked files. He pulled the thick Bellamy file toward him, then straightened and reorganized the rest, shifting the stack to the right a few inches. Not only did this make room for his lunch, the process also grounded him.

With the desk properly cleared, he opened the Krazyfish box and laid out his lunch. Jordan had had the foresight to pack the pie in its own container inside the box, which surprised Evan. And, he was very glad she did. Her ambush hug had dumped the contents of his taco into his coconut shrimp, which was a tragedy, but not beyond mitigation. He opened the dessert box and was relieved to see that the Key Lime pie wasn't one of the ridiculously green fakes pawned off on unsuspecting tourists.

The tacos were surprisingly good, if somewhat messy. He ate with his left hand, leaning over the box for each bite, as he flipped through the Bellamy file with his right.

The first file contained pretty much every bit of data available on Jacob Bellamy in the public record, which turned out to be a significant pile of paper. As a successful insurance middle-manager, Jake had his personal finances well organized. He had a retirement account in the early stages of development, a few thousand in savings, a little less in checking. The income was stable, the expenditures were modest and uninteresting. Beyond the house, his only debts were two low-balance credit cards and an auto loan for one of their vehicles. The other vehicle had been paid off a year ago. The file held statements from savings accounts and college funds he had established for both of his daughters. He had a healthy life insurance policy but, unless he was a complete ass, it wasn't enough to be killed for. If money had been the motive, he was worth far more alive than dead.

Of course, if the wife was running around on him, that would be a different story. Evan popped a shrimp in his mouth, crunching through the coconut crust, and considered the widow Bellamy. Nothing about her reaction gave any reason for Evan to suspect her. That didn't mean she was cleared – some people were better actors than Danny Coyle – but the feel of the whole encounter testified against her involvement. A stay-at-home mom in a new town was very unlikely to have the time, energy, interest, or availability to start an affair, fall so deep and so hard for the new guy as to conspire to kill her husband, all while keeping her house tidy and her kids well-behaved.

He opened Karen's file beside Jake's. Her finances were just as stable and uninteresting as his. She had no accounts listed under her maiden name. She had no accounts with a billing address different from her home address. The officer who had compiled this report stated that none of her social media activity seemed suspicious. Evan flipped a tab on Jake's file and saw a similar note about *his* social media accounts. Neither had any criminal history or civil suits. This was a first marriage for both of them. None of the obvious motives jumped out at him.

Karen had provided names of everyone Jake interacted with on a regular basis in the Port St. Joe area, as well as his boss and coworkers back in Tallahassee. Vi had processed about a dozen of these names and stuffed printouts into individual files for each. Evan flipped through these as he finished his shrimp, not really expecting to find anything but to lay a foundation for the investigation to come.

By the time the tacos and shrimp were gone and the pie was looking tasty, he had skimmed everything on his desk. He had highlighted one or two items for deeper consideration later, but for the most part, it seemed like Jake Bellamy had no enemies, had no addictions or compulsions, had no high-risk behaviors or associates. According to the reports, there was no reason for Jake to be dead.

Evan closed the files and reorganized them on the left side of his desk. He shut the box containing the remnants of his lunch and set it aside, and pulled the pie closer to him. He had just lifted his fork to take a bite when his direct line rang. On the second ring, he answered.

"Caldwell."

"This is Vi," said a voice that would have made Churchill jealous.

"Yes, Vi, what can I do for you?"

"Mr. Caldwell," she replied. It was never Sheriff, never Evan. He was okay with that. "Go home."

He stared at the phone for a moment, trying to figure out how to respond, or how she had known he was there, or whether she had the authority to tell him to go home. In the background, he heard the faint strains of Crosby, Stills & Nash singing *Southern Cross,* one of his favorites, and a cat meowing plaintively. For just a second, he wondered if she was on his boat. Before he could ask her, she had hung up.

With the lunch hour past and Monday approaching, the marina had quieted down significantly by the time Evan got home. Boaters visiting for the weekend from other points Floridian were packing up and pulling out. The Dockside Grill had quieted, its crowd reduced to just the full-time liveaboards relaxing with a beer or cocktail, and non-boating tourists having one last snack or drink before hitting the road.

By the time he was halfway down his pier, Evan had decided that he'd be happier cleaning up the boat while out on the bay than he would sitting there in the marina, so he changed out of his work clothes, threw on some cargo pants and a long-sleeved tee shirt, and prepared to get out on the water for the first time in too many days.

He usually took the fishing boat out when he wanted to get on the water. It was a 2001 Sea Fox 257 center console that he'd bought used from a RICO sale back in Brevard. He'd sold his car and kept Hannah's Pilot because it was paid for, but he'd hung onto the Sea Fox for his mental health. Today, he wanted to take the whole house out. He hadn't done so since he'd anchored out in the bay for a weekend, over a month ago, so he went through his checklist carefully before firing up the engines. Sarah got his lines for him but declined to go out with him when he'd invited her. She was studying for her ACT, and he figured that was as good a reason as she could have.

It was a windless day, and there was almost no chop to the bay. Evan was in no hurry to be anywhere specific, and he kept the Chris-Craft at fifteen knots or so. She topped out at thirty, but he'd only run her that fast once, to get the cobwebs out.

Once he was out in the bay proper, he saw that the cool weather had kept most people on land. There were only a few other boats out; a small ketch that was on the hook, and a few sport fishers looking for redfish or just an excuse to kick back with a few beers.

Evan decided to take her around the northern tip of the peninsula into the Gulf and had just changed his heading when he saw a flash of black down in the open hatch located over the V-berth. It was gone, and then it was back, and Plutes slid out of the hatch and walked toward the bow.

Evan cursed under his breath, put engine one in reverse, effectively shifting into neutral, then jumped from the ladder down to the aft deck, tossed himself over the rail to the deck below, and made his way along the starboard side as quickly as he could.

When he got to the bow, Plutes was sitting pretty as you please, between the open hatch and the windlass. He turned his head regally as he heard Evan approach, then flattened his ears and ran to the port side as Evan got closer. Evan waited for him to slide off and into the water, which would heap even more coals of spousal guilt onto his head, but the cat kept his footing and disappeared around the corner. Evan followed.

The cat was gone by the time he made the port side. Evan hadn't heard a splash, but he looked over the side anyway before hurrying to the aft deck. There was no sign of Plutes there, and Evan mentally kicked himself for forgetting to close the forward hatch as he again walked forward on the starboard side. Plutes was back on the bow, sitting tall like he was waiting for fireworks to start. Evan got to within a foot of the cat before it looked over its shoulder, but Evan managed to scoop him up anyway.

"What the hell's wrong with you?" he muttered, newly surprised at how heavy Plutes actually was. He took him through the salon and down to the V-berth. Evan used the room for storage since he never had guests; mainly plastic totes of Hannah's belongings stacked neatly on the full-sized berth. Evan could see that it was an easy twelve inches or so from the top of the tallest tote to the hatch. He dropped Plutes on an empty spot on the berth, then reached up and secured the hatch.

On his way back out, he double-checked that all of the windows were closed, then made sure to close the glass door behind him. He couldn't help thinking that it would be just like his life for him to lose the cat in the Gulf a week before his wife finally awoke. Somehow, in his imagination, it was the cat she asked for first. Then he felt ashamed, because, contrary to the implications made by her affair, he knew Hannah loved him.

Once Evan had dropped anchor and spent about an hour on routine cleaning, he fell into a peaceful state close to meditation. The mindless rhythm of the work, the gentle lap of the water against the hull, the occasional cry of a gull, all worked to calm his mind. He spent half his time focusing on the facts of the Bellamy case, and the other half trying not to think about it.

It was close to five by the time he'd finished work, had a cup of coffee on the aft deck, and then gone ahead and pulled anchor. As he made his way back along the port side toward the bridge ladder, he passed Plutes sitting on top of the teak built-in, staring out the window. The cat gave him a baleful look as he passed.

EIGHT

MONDAY MORNING, Evan and Goff sat across the desk from each other in Evan's office, sipping hot beverages. Both beverages could be called 'coffee,' but one likely wouldn't recognize the other if they met in the wild. Evan's travel mug transported his *café con leche* in style and comfort. Goff's drink felt right at home in a paper cup. It was as black and occluded as old motor oil, but he claimed to enjoy it.

Three copies of the Jake Bellamy file sat in a neat stack between them. Evan had asked Vi to make duplicate files so that each team member would have one. The master file would be retained in Evan's office and updated each morning with the prior day's developments.

"So, got off the phone with Trigg a few minutes ago," Evan said. "She got DNA from under his nails, mostly his own and someone who's a familial match. She's going to swab the wife and kids later today, just in case he has a cousin who hates him, but it'll probably turn out to be one of theirs. There was one other sample, but it's not in the system, so no help until we have a suspect. Ditto the fiber she pulled from his zipper pull. Nothing to match it to."

"What about the shoe prints?" Goff asked, sipping a chunk of coffee.

"A lot of his, and several partials of another athletic shoe. Size men's eleven, and the tread is an Adidas model, I forget which one. One of the moderate shoes, nothing fancy. Again, something that'll be handier later than it is now, if we get lucky." He took a last swallow of his coffee and pulled a legal pad toward him. "Okay, let's nail down the rest of this team."

"Well, Jimmy Crenshaw'd be an obvious choice, I figure, seeing as he and I have been with it from the beginning," Goff said.

"He's a good deputy," Evan considered. "A little too intense at times. Do you think he's up for it?"

"Well, sure. If you pair him with the right partner."

"Okay, I'll put him with you."

Goff sputtered into his drink, then coughed and said, "I wasn't referring to me. Hook him up with Peters or Holland. Those guys'll keep him in line."

"I can't put both senior sergeants on the same case. If you're in, Peters is out," Evan said. "And Holland is out because he's Holland."

Goff snorted. "Not your biggest fan, is he?"

"He's a much better deputy when he doesn't remember I'm in charge," Evan said. "He's just fine when he's reporting to you or Peters, but I have a feeling he wouldn't be much good working in a small unit that reports directly to me."

Goff was nodding and grinning. He looked up at Evan as if about to say something, but then took a long slurp of his coffee instead.

After he had swallowed and still did not have anything to say, Evan tried again. "You, Crenshaw, myself, and one other deputy. Who would you recommend?"

Goff looked over Evan's shoulder at the BOLO board, his eyes roving across the various photos. Evan thought his expression held more of an eenie-meenie-miny-moe vibe than thoughtful consideration. He also figured it might not be easy to take him too seriously while staring at the BOLO board.

Eventually, Goff said, "Go with Meyers. He's lived in this town his whole life. Only time he's ever been gone is when he was at FSU. Comes from a family that's been around long as I can remember. He's about the same age as our victim. In fact, his kids probably go to school with the Bellamy kids."

Evan liked Colin Meyers well enough, as much as he knew him. The deputy was about thirty-five, of average height and build, with light brown hair he kept cut close. He tended to blend into the woodwork in a group situation, but once he opened his mouth his intelligence was clear.

"Meyers it is," Evan agreed, hoping they could get through the rest of the day's business a bit more expeditiously. "Give him and Jimmy a shout on the radio. Call them in and we'll start building a strategy."

Evan, Goff, Meyers, and Crenshaw met half an hour later in a room that was sometimes the conference room, sometimes the break room, and sometimes the storage room, depending on the needs of the moment. It had once also served as the college football room, but the small flat-screen TV that had given it that name had belonged to Hutchens. His family's representative had collected it along with the rest of Hutch's belongings.

Evan handed identical files to each member of his team, which had been given the grandiose title of the Bellamy Task Force. After allowing several minutes for the team to familiarize themselves with the contents of the files, Evan made assignments. He and Goff would go through the files Vi had put together on the contacts list, then they had an appointment to chat with Mr. Bellamy's boss.

Meyers and Crenshaw, much to their dismay, would start shoveling through the phone records. Evan had acquired call lists from Jake's personal and business cell phones, Jake's home and office phones, and Karen Bellamy's cell phone. He wanted a name attached to every incoming and outgoing call on each line, and he wanted biographical information attached to each of those names, if they hadn't already been pulled by Vi from the contact list Karen had given them.

"When you say, 'biographical information,'" Crenshaw asked, "just how much of their life story do you want?"

"Where they live, what they do for work, what is their connection to our victim, what were they calling about – if you can find out from the widow or someone at the insurance agency without contacting the individual. I don't want you guys making contact with any of these people yet. If you can't find anything in public records or a quick internet search, just note that and move on. This is a lot of ground to cover," Evan said, nodding to the phone records. "We want to sketch the picture as quick as we can, then fill in the details as time allows."

"This *is* a lot of ground to cover," Meyers said. "Why'd I get stuck with phone records again?"

"'Cause you did such a fine job last time," Goff said. "And Crenshaw, in case you were wondering the same thing, it's 'cause you need the experience." The bristly ends of Goff's mustache popped up in an imitation smile.

"Not complaining," Meyers said, "just wondering."

"Well, now you know," Goff said.

"Now I know," Meyers agreed, and made an exaggerated show of lifting the heavy stack of phone records.

"How 'bout you follow me back to my cubicle, Jimmy, and I'll show you how it's done."

"Can't wait," Crenshaw said. His tone was sarcastic, but Evan could tell the young deputy was excited to be assigned to the task force.

· ● ✳ ● ·

Evan and Goff pulled into Seminole Insurance just after noon. Bellamy's boss, Carl Nelson, was waiting for them in the lobby. He was a large man, wearing a tan suit that had gone out of style twenty years ago but had been manufactured much more recently. Evan wondered where you could even buy a suit like that, or why you would want to.

Nelson shook their hands and welcomed them to his place of business. He had a red face and wispy blond hair that had been combed into a graceful swoop to conceal his shiny scalp.

He led them to his desk at the back of the office. It was dark wood polished to a high gloss, but its surface was almost completely covered by files and stacks of paperwork. An impressive blue swordfish hung on the wall behind his desk, with a plaque below it that said, "The Big One."

"I just don't know what to tell you," Nelson said as he settled into his high-backed leather chair. "Jake was such a nice guy, I can't imagine why anyone would want to hurt him."

Evan and Goff sat across from him. Their chairs were also heavily cushioned black leather, but not quite as impressive as Nelson's. From where they sat, the "Big One" plaque hung just above Nelson's gleaming scalp. It appeared to be a comment on the man rather than his trophy.

Nelson asked, "Do you think it could have been a random thing? I mean, maybe one of these kids on LSD or something? Or one of those crazy psycho killers, like on TV?" His eyes grew wider with his speculations.

"Mr. Nelson," Evan said, "we're in the very early stages of this investigation. I'm afraid we have more questions than answers right now."

"I just can't believe…I mean, it seems like if anybody was going to get killed, Jake would have been the last guy I'd have thought it would be."

"So, he never had any arguments with any of his coworkers?" Evan asked.

Nelson guffawed, "No! That's what I'm trying to tell you. There'd have to be something really wrong with you to not like Jake. I don't mean he was a limp-wrist, Casper Milktoast type. He seemed like a solid guy, just, he didn't get upset too easy, and he never really upset anybody else."

"His wife said that he went out to dinner and drinks with some guys from the office recently. Were you with him that night?" Evan asked.

"Oh, yes. We try to do that with all the new guys, you know, once they've settled in here. You know, just to let them know that they're part of the team. It helps them get to know who we are as a business, and who we are as a community."

"Where did you go that night?" Evan asked.

"Krazyfish," Nelson said, a hint of a contented smile lighting his face as if he were reliving the experience. "Jordan was our waitress. She'll probably remember us."

Evan sighed. If Jordan had information they needed, he'd assign that interview to Goff. He asked, "Did anything happen that night? Any altercations at all, maybe with someone not associated with your company?"

Nelson shook his head. "No. It was a quiet night. We had some fish. We had some drinks. Nothing out of the ordinary. Ginger, she's the receptionist you just met, Ginger's pregnant, so she wasn't drinking. That's who drove us all home, Sheriff, I swear." He smiled to indicate he was joshing just a little.

Evan wasn't sure that making the pregnant lady drive all the drunk men home was something to brag about, but he guessed it was better than the drunks driving themselves.

"Can you tell us what he had been working on over the last couple weeks?" he asked.

"Well, he was just coming up to speed, trying to straighten out Babcock's old files," Nelson said. "Babcock had been with us for several years, but we had to let him go a few months back. Turns out he was playing a little fast and loose with the old rules of conduct...if you know what I mean."

"I guess I don't know what you mean," Evan said. "What exactly did he do?"

"Oh, nothing illegal, per se. He just kinda slipped a few extra riders onto policies here and there. Sold folks insurance they didn't need, and couldn't have actually used even if they knew they had it," Nelson said. "He had all sorts of ways of maximizing his production numbers, and none of his little tricks were in the best interest of his clients. Or Seminole Insurance. So, we kindly asked him to leave, then contacted the insurance commissioner and got his license yanked."

"And then you brought in Bellamy to replace him?" Evan asked.

Nelson's eyes widened. He started shaking his head and moving his lips a second or two before he actually spoke. "Now," he said, raising his hands off the desk a bit, "now, don't get any half-cocked ideas. Babcock was gone long before we brought Jake in. He never met Jake. It wasn't like Jake took his spot or anything."

"Mr. Nelson," Evan asked, "do you know where we can contact Mr. Babcock?"

"Sure. But, I'm telling you, I don't see how Babcock could have thought it was Jake's fault. I mean, if he was gonna kill somebody, wouldn't he have come after me? I'm the one that fired him, not Jake."

"Like I said, we are in the very early stages. We need to look at everything," Evan said. "Often it's the things people disregard that end up breaking a case. We'll find Mr. Babcock and have a word with him. What was his first name?"

"Phil," Nelson said.

"Phil Babcock," Evan said as he scribbled the name in his notepad. "As far as Babcock's files that Bellamy was trying to straighten out, has there been any unusual activity with any of those accounts?"

"What do you mean by unusual?" Nelson asked.

"Any large insurance buys? Any unusual claims? Any recent claims denied? Angry customers? Anything like that?"

Nelson was shaking his head again, but slowly. "I guess I'll have to look through them. Babcock did a pretty good job of hiding some of that stuff, so the files were a mess when he left. I sicced Jake on them, but I don't know how much he managed to straighten out. I guess that's going to be my work for today…and tomorrow," he said, nodding glumly toward the piles of paperwork on his desk. "I'd offer to let you see them, but those files are confidential. You'd either need a warrant or client consent for me to show them to you."

Evan pulled his card from his jacket pocket and slid it across the crowded desk. "Just keep your eyes out for anything unusual as you go through those. Give me a call if something catches your eye, or if you remember anything else."

"Certainly," Nelson said, and stood up. He reached his hand across to shake Evan's.

Evan interpreted the gesture to mean Nelson was ready for them to leave. Evan wasn't. "I do need you to give me your last known address and phone number for Phil Babcock."

Nelson straightened and held up a finger. "Babcock, right." He punched a button on his phone, activating the intercom. A female voice answered. Nelson said, "Ginger, get Babcock's personnel file. I need all his contact info."

A moment later a petite redhead popped into the office holding a file card. She looked like she had a beach ball stuffed under her shirt. Her name tag said Llewellyn. Evan realized that Ginger was a nickname, and not a particularly inventive one. He decided not to comment on this just then.

Nelson accepted the card, thanked and dismissed her. Then he gave the card to Evan. "I really don't think he's got anything to do with this. I doubt you're going to find him at this address either. I've heard he left town as soon as I fired him, but I don't know that for sure."

"Thank you, Mr. Nelson," Evan said. "We'll find him and have a word."

· ● ✳ ● ·

"You think maybe one of this Babcock character's customers held a grudge?" Goff asked as they drove back to the office.

"How do you mean?" Evan asked.

"He got the ax for ripping off his customers. Maybe one of them decided to balance the books, but carved their pound of flesh off the wrong insurance man?"

Evan looked sideways at Goff.

"It's a reach," Goff admitted, "but it wouldn't be the craziest thing I ever saw. Say you found out your insurance man was skimming money out of your grandbaby's college fund. Say your dad died and you find out that the life insurance he's been paying for his whole life isn't enough to cover his widow's property tax and the state takes her house all because your insurance man, who you've never met, had sold him an empty policy." Goff popped a stick of Big Red into his mouth and chewed a moment. "That might be reason enough to get your dander up. A guy in that place might go looking for the pile of poo that sold his parents a bill of goods. How is he to know that the account has changed hands?"

"You're right, it is a big reach," Evan said. "But, it's as good as anything else we have."

"I think Fish Man was right about Babcock," Goff said. "He isn't much of a suspect."

"What are you thinking?"

"I've been doing this a long time. Seen more than enough killings to know that whoever killed that man, he was just about as mad as a person is likely to get," Goff said.

"I think you're right about that," Evan agreed. "The problem is, we can't find anyone who had any reason to be mad at Bellamy."

Goff nodded. "That's what I'm saying. Seems like Babcock would go for Nelson before he would Bellamy."

"Yeah, but right now we have to look under even the littlest rocks," Evan said as he stopped for a red light.

After grabbing a quick lunch at the Indian Pass Raw Bar Uptown (no comparison to the original, more atmospherically-friendly place out on 30, according to Goff), Evan dropped Goff back off at the office and switched him out for Meyers.

They pulled out and headed for Hwy 98, which ran along the bay. The Babcocks lived in a neighborhood at the northern end of Port St. Joe.

According to the file they'd pulled on Babcock, toying with people's insurance policies wasn't his first toe-dip into trouble. Back in the 90s, he'd been charged with assault with a deadly weapon. It had been downgraded to simple assault, but it still made Babcock more interesting than anyone else so far.

"You think we should call first?" Colin Meyers asked. "Middle of a Monday, he might not be home."

"That could be to our advantage. We might get a chance to talk to his wife before either of them knows why we're there. Maybe she'll let something slip," Evan said. "Besides, it's a short drive. If nobody's home, we'll just come back."

Meyers nodded and took a drink of the soda he'd brought with him. They drove in silence for a few minutes and then turned right on 98. Evan's attention was caught by the Cape San Blas Lighthouse ahead, and to their left. The original brick tower had been destroyed twice by hurricanes. It had been replaced with a skeletal steel structure and rebuilt or moved half a dozen times since the war between the states, as erosion swallowed more and more of the peninsula. Now, it sat safely inland, no longer guiding lost ships, but providing a small glimpse of the area's past and, for those spry enough to climb the hundred feet to its watch room, an impressive view of its present.

The lighthouse eventually left Evan's rearview, and they continued through a fairly barren section of Hwy 98, dotted with the odd boat repair shop or warehouse until they hit the George G Tapper Bridge. Once on the other side of the water, Hwy 98 became FL-30, and they entered a more residential area. They took the first turn after the bridge onto Dolphin Street, which took them into a quiet neighborhood of small, older homes.

"I never even knew this neighborhood was out here," Evan said.

"My aunt and her kids live out this way, about a mile further north," Meyers said.

As they continued along Dolphin, past a church, a small park, and several yards housing modest boats on trailers, the road narrowed, and the houses became newer and larger, though not fancy by anyone's definition.

"Expensive out here?" Evan asked.

"Like everything else, it depends on when you bought it," Meyers answered with a shrug. "Nowhere near as bad as in town, or down to Cape San Blas, though."

"I wonder how much of a hardship losing his job has been for this guy," Evan said, as they passed a fenced yard where two toddlers argued over a Little Tykes truck.

"He's probably okay," Meyers said. "House is paid for."

"You know him?" Evan asked.

"I know her," Meyers answered. "From high school. Not real well, but enough to talk to at the last reunion. Her mom came into some life insurance, gave Cindy and him the money for the house a few years back."

"Makes you wonder why a guy with a paid off house is stupid enough to do what he did."

"I think stupid's the key word, there," Meyers said. "That and arrogance. The guy didn't make much of an impression on me when she introduced us. Twelve-oh-one, guess that's it on the left."

The Babcock residence was a ranch with a fake stone front and dark-stained wood trim. It looked like thousands of other bland, contractor-designed houses, but it was well kept. A sedan and a fairly-new pickup occupied the open two-car garage.

"Looks like he might be home after all," Meyers said.

Evan pulled into the driveway and eyed the house.

"You thinking he might try to run?" Meyers asked.

"If he does, he's an idiot," Evan said. "We don't have anything on him yet."

"It'd make our job a lot easier," Meyers said.

Evan thought it might take Meyers a minute or two to get his big frame up to speed, but he also decided he'd never want a guy that size chasing him.

"Tell you what," Evan said, "let's just go knock on the door and see what happens."

What happened was, a pretty blonde woman in her mid-thirties answered the door with a baby on her hip. She seemed mildly annoyed when she saw Meyer's uniform, then smiled when she looked at his face.

"Hey. Carter Meyers, right?"

"Colin."

"Right." Her smile faded as she looked Evan over, but she didn't look particularly worried. He introduced himself, and she expressed shock and mock modesty that the actual sheriff himself would drive all the way across the bridge just to talk to lil' ol' her.

"You know," she said, with an impressive eyeroll, "Nelson and Seminole made a pretty nice chunk of change off those policies. Probably just as much as we got. I didn't see him refunding any of that money."

"Ma'am," Evan said, "That's not what we're here about. Is Mr. Babcock home? We'd like to speak with him if we could."

"He's busy," she said. "Haven't we been through enough already?"

Before Evan could respond, Meyers spoke up. "Cindy, we need to ask your husband some questions about something totally different. It's serious. Please go get Phillip."

She glared at him for a moment, then finally said, "Well, you might as well sit on the sofa so you don't let all the damn heat out." She flapped her free arm in the general direction of the living room, then marched toward the back of the house.

Evan raised an eyebrow at Meyers, Meyers nodded at Evan, and the two of them entered, closing the door behind them, and moved into the living room. They did not sit, however, but stood near the picture window as they waited for Babcock to make an appearance.

After a few minutes, and a few harsh words muffled by a closed door, he did. He was a tall man with a sharp nose and a slightly hen-pecked appearance. He wore khakis and a polo shirt and was barefoot. Clearly not getting ready for a job interview.

"Now what?" he asked, more resigned than antagonistic.

"Mr. Babcock," Evan said, "I'm Sheriff Caldwell, this is Deputy Meyers. We need to ask you a couple questions."

Babcock motioned to the couch, then sat heavily in a plush recliner. Evan and Meyers settled at either end of the sofa. From somewhere down the hall, Cindy yelled, "I'm putting the baby down, so keep it quiet out there."

"What kind of questions?" Babcock asked, paying no mind to his wife.

"You were recently let go from Seminole Mutual, correct?" Evan asked.

Babcock nodded.

"Can you tell us about that?" Evan asked.

"No," Babcock said. "I didn't do anything illegal, I just had a different interpretation on some of the company's guidelines. But, my lawyer says I'm not supposed to talk about it, just to be safe. If this is about that, you'll need to talk to him, not me."

"How long ago was that?" Evan asked.

"Well," Babcock said, turning to look out the front picture window at the stark blue sky, "we're sitting here in the middle of January, and they sent me packing end of October. So…two, two-and-a-half months? You can do the math."

Evan nodded. Beside him, Meyers scribbled notes on a pad. Evan asked, "Mr. Babcock, without divulging anything that might get your lawyer cross, can you think of anybody who might be upset at you? A client, or perhaps someone up the chain from you at Seminole?"

"Shoot, everybody at Seminole was upset at me, pretty much all the time," Babcock said dismissively. "First they were mad because I wasn't selling enough. Then they were mad because I was selling too much."

"What about your clients?" Evan asked. "After you were let go, did you get any threatening calls or letters?"

Babcock sat up a bit straighter, leaned forward and narrowed his eyes. "No," he said slowly. "Why are you here? This isn't about insurance, is it? Something else is going on."

"Yes, it is," Evan said. "I want you to think very carefully. Did you receive threats of any kind in the last few months of your employment at Seminole Mutual, or after leaving there?"

"What do you mean?'" Babcock asked. Evan noticed that his wife, Cindy, had silently slipped back into earshot just inside the hall. Her nostrils flared slightly, and her eyes were keen.

Evan said nothing, He let the gravity of his previous question hang in the air.

After a moment, Babcock said, "No, I didn't get any threats. I mean, nothing serious. Every once in a while, we get some ridiculous claim and the customer thinks he can bully his way around the facts, you know, and when that doesn't work, they usually make a lot of noise, but nothing ever comes of it."

"Has that happened recently?" Evan asked.

Babcock looked back to the window, thinking. Eventually, he shook his head. "No, not that I can recall." He paused, then asked, "What are you talking about?"

Meyers said, "How many times you been arrested, Mr. Babcock?"

"What?" he said, turning his head and cocking it slightly. "I didn't get arrested. I told you, I got fired, but I didn't do anything illegal."

"So," Meyers said, flipping through his notepad, "you've never been arrested?"

"Well, once, but that was twenty years ago," Babcock said. "Maybe more."

"Twenty-two years," Evan said. "You attacked someone up in Tallahassee. What can you tell us about that?"

"What? I didn't attack... Listen," he leaned forward and licked his lips. "Listen, I don't know what you heard, or what they told you, but that was just kid stuff. A bunch of us got into a ruckus at a college football game. The cops had to break it up, but it was really no big deal."

"Assault with a deadly weapon *is* a big deal, Mr. Babcock," Meyers said.

Babcock flopped back in his chair and let out an exasperated sigh. "What is it that you want? Yes, I got fired. Yes, I got arrested once for being a drunk football fan. No, I can't think of any other publicly humiliating events in my life for you to ask me about. So, if there's nothing else, I'd like to get back to my job search." He gestured in the direction of the bedroom.

"What was the deadly weapon?" Meyers asked.

"It wasn't a weapon, it was a beer bottle," Babcock said. "And it wasn't deadly, that's why they dropped the charges."

"Also, because your mom was sleeping with the district attorney," Cindy said from the hall.

"*Really*, Cindy!" Babcock said, "Do you really need to bring that up now?"

"It's the truth, ain't it?" she said. "That's what they're here for. Just the facts, ma'am. Right?"

"They're not here to ask who my mom was sleeping with," Babcock said, craning his neck around to look down the hall at her. "You want me to start giving them the *facts* about your sister?"

"Wait a minute!" Evan said, holding up a hand. "Let's try to stay on one topic at a time, okay?" He looked at Cindy until she sighed and slumped her shoulders, then turned back to her husband. "Mr. Babcock, do you keep in touch with your former coworkers at Seminole?"

"No, why would I? They all acted like they were so much more ethical than me."

Evan reached into his jacket and pulled out a copy of Jake Bellamy's license photo. He held it out to Babcock. "Do you know this man?"

Babcock took the photo. "No, why? Is this the guy you think might be after me?"

Evan took the picture back from him. "No, he's the man who replaced you."

Babcock shrugged. "So, what does he have to do with anything? I hope he's very happy with Nelson and the rest of those idiots."

"He's not. He's dead."

Babcock's eyes widened. His wife suddenly appeared back in the doorway. "Who's dead?"

Evan kept his eyes on Babcock, whose mouth had dropped open just a bit.

"Is that why you think someone is after me?"

"I didn't say anyone was," Evan said. "We're just looking at all possibilities, including those related to Seminole."

"Well…I'm not related to Seminole anymore."

"Where were you early Saturday morning?" Evan asked him.

"How early?"

"Between five and seven."

"I was at the Homewood Suites in Pensacola," Babcock answered. "I checked out after breakfast, around eight."

"What were you doing there?"

"Why?"

"Please just answer the question, sir."

"I was visiting my brother. He wanted me to come work with him in his construction company."

Evan looked at Babcock's wife, still standing in the doorway. "Were you with him, ma'am?"

"No. I hate those people. His whole family's a bunch of rednecks."

"Cindy—" Babcock started.

"Wait a minute," she said, ignoring him. "Is this about the guy that got stabbed?"

"Who got stabbed?" Babcock asked, like he was losing the thread of the conversation.

"Yes, this man is the man who was killed Saturday morning," Evan said. Babcock wasn't their guy. "So, you were here alone Saturday morning?" Evan asked the wife.

"Yeah. I mean, the kids were with me." She popped a fist onto her hip. "So?"

Evan stood up. Meyers seemed a little surprised by this but was just one beat behind him.

"You folks probably don't have anything to worry about," Evan said. "Like I said, we're just trying to cover all the bases."

"Well, are we in danger, or what?" Babcock asked.

"Probably not," Evan answered. "Just be aware and let us know if anything makes you nervous."

By the looks on their faces, Evan was the one making them nervous. He didn't care; he'd been, he'd heard, he was ready to go.

Five minutes later, they pulled out of the Babcocks' driveway.

"When we get back to the office, check with Homewood Suites and see when he checked out."

"You think he might have done it?" Meyers asked.

"No, I don't. He seemed pretty convinced that we were there because *he* was at risk. He could be a good actor, but I doubt it." Evan pulled his visor down. The sun was like needles at this time of day. "Also, there's no way he wears a size eleven shoe. He's a nine at best."

"Man, I didn't even look," Meyers said, slapping his thigh. "You know, if I was a bad guy in this situation, I'd go buy a pair of shoes two sizes too big and stuff 'em."

"Yeah, but you're smart," Evan said. "As much as I would like Babcock to be our guy, he just isn't that bright."

NINE

LATE IN THE AFTERNOON, Evan pulled into the Gulf County Medical Examiner's Office. It was a small, tan building that could pass for a dentist or accountant's office if someone didn't catch the unobtrusive sign. The sign itself was practically camouflaged, as if by hiding the ME's office, the county could convince residents that there were, in fact, no dead people in town.

Evan was waved through to the back, where he found Danny looming over a stainless-steel table. A small iPhone speaker on the counter beside him was playing something by The Buggles. Evan had never been a big fan, so he couldn't remember the song, but it wasn't what he would have expected, either from Danny or the morgue.

There were three other tables in the room. Two were empty and one held a body covered with an opaque plastic sheet. The feet of the body over which Danny was laboring were facing Evan and he could see that they were small and wrinkled; clearly not Bellamy.

"What have you got there, Danny?" Evan asked.

The kid jumped just enough to notice, but he smiled when he looked up at Evan. "Oh, hey, Sheriff!" he said, then exchanged his smile for a look of sorrow, which was sincere despite its speed. "Neighbor found this poor little lady dead in her La-Z-Boy yesterday. It's looking like heart failure."

"Probably as good a way as any," Evan said, then took a sip from his bottled water.

"Right?" Danny asked. He started pulling off his gloves. "I have serious phobias now about how I don't want to die, right? For instance, I'm definitely not in favor of either a motorcycle or automobile accident, in particular, anything involving one of those flatbeds full of lumber or big iron pipes. I don't have to worry about plunging to a fiery death from the sky because I don't fly—Jesus said 'Lo, I am with you always,' so I stay on the ground, you know?"

Evan didn't bother agreeing or disagreeing. He just drank his water as he watched the kid toss his gloves in the biohazard can nearby and pull another pair out of a box on the counter.

"I'm also against dying from TB, any kind of worm or other squirmy parasite, Ebola, and testicular cancer."

Danny pulled the plastic sheet up over the old woman and headed for the other occupied table. Evan followed.

"This is my second year, right, and I also did some volunteer medic work in Haiti, the DR, and Mexico. As a consequence, I've got a long list of CODs that give me nightmares, you follow?"

"I do."

Danny leaned on the table that Evan presumed held Jake Bellamy and sighed. "It should go without saying that stabbing is in the vicinity of the top of that list. If it wasn't already, it would be now."

"Bellamy's pretty bad," Evan commiserated.

"Right?" Danny asked, his expression one of dramatic relief, like everyone else he'd talked to had disagreed. "So, speaking of Jacob, he's a mess."

Danny pulled the plastic sheeting down and folded it just above Bellamy's knees. Evan no longer cringed at the sight of a body sporting the enormous Y-incision made for autopsy, but he couldn't help wincing at the sight of Jake Bellamy. One would think that a victim looked much worse covered in blood, but in fact, once the body was cleaned up and its wounds were left bare, it was much more appalling, at least to Evan.

"Yeah, so—oh, hey!" Danny cocked his head like he'd just heard his mom calling him, then started doing some weird jerky thing. For just a second, Evan was surprised to think that Danny was epileptic, but then he realized he was just dancing.

"Johnny…" he sang along in a breathy voice. "Riding on the monorail…"

He stopped jerking as abruptly as he'd started and looked down at Bellamy. "My favorite. So, anyway, Jacob did not have an easy death." He grabbed what looked like a long pair of tweezers and started tapping gently at the cluster of narrow wounds on Bellamy's torso. "As you can see, we have nine separate stab wounds here, with several overlapping. Judging by blood loss and tissue samples, I'm going to wager that he was alive for at least the majority of these. At least three wounds would have killed him at some point on their own. They punctured the liver. But he could also have died eventually from a combination of blood loss and two punctures to the upper right lobe of the lungs."

"Okay," Evan said, then took a drink.

"Meanwhile, as you saw Saturday, we have numerous defensive wounds on the hands, both back and front, including a through and through in the left palm. The rest of the wounds to the hands and forearms are slicing motions. Only one of them has any real depth to it."

"What does that tell you?" Evan asked.

"Oh, well, he definitely wasn't in the mood to die," Danny said without humor. "He put up a good fight. I find it interesting that there weren't any slashes on the torso, though."

"I think you said that at the scene," Evan said.

"Yeah. Because you would think if someone was fighting back, that the killer would just be swinging wild, right? Because to me, this doesn't look like a seriously organized thing. He just hammered away here until the guy was dead, but the stab wounds themselves are pretty concentrated."

Evan didn't disagree, though he wasn't sure it meant anything, except that it wasn't a professional hit or even a very experienced killer. His impression was that there was a lot of anger, and maybe even fear, behind the frenzy of wounds. "What can you tell me about the weapon?"

"Well, measurements of the wounds tell me you're looking for an eight-inch, very narrow blade. Also, based on the nicks to the fifth and sixth ribs that correlate with two of the flesh wounds, it's a double-edged blade. So, I'm thinking switchblade. A stiletto, actually. No flaws or deviations I could find, so I would say the blade is new or has been extremely well cared for and maintained."

"Okay," Evan said. "What can you tell me about the person wielding it? Anything?"

"Oh, sure. Based on the angles of trajectory, bruising around the wounds, and depth, I'd say you're definitely looking at a man, right-handed, and Bellamy's height or just a bit taller. And not a nice person by anyone's definition."

"Any idea how long this struggle took?"

Danny looked down at Bellamy's chest and sighed. "No more than a minute, maybe two. His heart had already stopped beating by the time the guy rolled him down the embankment."

Evan thought this might explain why no one heard any cries for help. Bellamy's focus would have been on fighting off the rapid-fire attacks of the knife, and he'd have been dead before he had a moment to think.

Danny started bouncing on the balls of his feet, his head bobbing along just a bit. "Love the Buggles, right?"

Evan shook his head. "What year were you born?"

"Oh, ninety-one, right? But the eighties were it for music."

"You're older than you look," Evan said.

"Yeah, said every bartender I ever met," Danny said, still once more. He looked down at Bellamy, somewhat wistfully. "The music helps, right?" He looked back up at Evan. "I mean, you do what you need to do. You make a few jokes, you avoid looking at the faces, and you keep your music on." He pulled the sheet back up over Bellamy's body. "Otherwise, the world gets really scary and you develop phobias about all the ways you don't want to die, right?"

If Evan had been the hugging type, he might have hugged Danny then. "I use music a lot, too, Danny. And running. You might try running. It works for me."

The kid perked up again. "Oh, no, because you know those lizards that run on water? Yeah, that's me, so no." He blinked at Evan, his long, dark lashes almost making a thumping noise against his cheeks. "When it gets really bad, I go home and watch *Charlie Brown's Christmas*, and think about a time when a kid's world was that quiet and gentle, you know?"

Evan wasn't unkind enough to tell Danny it had never been like that, at least not in any world he'd inhabited. "Okay, listen, email me the full report, okay?"

"I'll make sure Grundy gets it to you," Danny said, snapping off his gloves. "I don't have access to email those reports. Just an intern, remember."

Evan watched him, unsure how to take his answer.

"Hey, I promise. You'll have it by end of day," Danny assured him.

"Okay, Danny, I believe you," Evan said. "I'll talk to you later."

Danny held up a hand in farewell and started back over to the old lady. Evan headed for the door. He was opening the door when he heard Danny.

"Oh, right! Billy Idol."

Evan turned around. The kid had his back to him and was bopping and jerking and singing along to "*Dancing with Myself.*" Evan let the door swing shut behind him and wondered if it was too early for a cocktail.

The day was so bright outside that Evan felt like he'd just entered another universe. It was jarring to go from staring at a violently dead body to looking at people window shopping and laughing on their phones. When Evan stopped for a red light in front of a big pet supply store, that seemed like as good a buffer as any, and he waited until his way was clear, changed lanes, and pulled into the parking lot.

He'd never had occasion to visit such a store, and he was amazed that a building about the size of a Home Depot could sell nothing but pet-related merchandise. How much stuff could a dog, cat, or guinea pig need?

He wandered down the center of the store, his head swerving left then right and back again as he read the signs over the aisles. One entire aisle was devoted to cat food, and he guessed that figured. The next aisle looked promisingly feline-oriented, and he slowly made his way along the shelves, squinting at objects that he didn't know existed or didn't recognize at all.

About halfway down the aisle, he picked up an object with a suction cup at one end, something that might be a furry shrimp at the other, and a springy stick in between. He was puzzling out its purpose when a young guy with shaggy blond hair and an optimistic sprinkling of mustache appeared beside him.

"Hi, welcome to Pet Warehouse," the kid said. "Can I help you with anything?"

Evan held up the stick with the furry shrimp, which bounced in front of the guy's face, "Yeah, what's this?"

"Oh, it's a toy. Very popular," the guy said with a huge, white smile. "Helps deter your cat from scratching the furniture, too."

That was one violation that Plutes hadn't visited upon Evan. "I see." He looked down toward the end of the aisle. "Do you have any, uh, what would you call them…harnesses? You know, a harness for a cat?"

"For a cat?" The guy frowned. "Well, not per se. We have several that will fit a small dog, but cats aren't usually too enthusiastic about going out for walks."

"No, this is for something else," Evan said.

"Okay, well, they're over here by the leashes," the guy said.

Evan followed him out of the aisle, bringing the furry shrimp thing with him. Two aisles down, the guy veered into an aisle with more leashes and collars and other apparatus than Evan thought was necessary.

"Here you go," the guy said, gesturing at a section of harnesses that varied in appearance from thongs to straightjackets. "How big is your kitty?"

Evan frowned, then spread his hands. "About so. He weighed twenty pounds at the vet."

"That's a big-un," the guy said, then pointed at a row near the floor. "These should be a good fit," he said.

Evan bent down and pulled one from its hook. His last foster father had worn something like it for his hernia.

"That's a nice one," the sales guy said. "Nice padding, for comfort. Do you need a leash?"

Evan nodded, and the guy grabbed one obviously designed to go with that halter.

Evan turned the halter over in his hand. "Do you have anything…I was thinking it would have a little more hardware."

"What kind of hardware?"

"Well, I don't know. Maybe I could add some. Maybe sew in some D-rings or something."

"What for?"

"I'm thinking maybe bungee cords," Evan said, frowning at the harness. The guy didn't answer, and kind of a long moment went by, so Evan looked up to see if the guy was still there. He was.

"Uh, for what, exactly?" he asked.

Evan realized he was thinking out loud too much, perhaps. "Well, to secure to my boat." He said quietly.

The guy blinked at him a few times.

"Hey, you're the sheriff, aren't you?" he asked finally.

There was no best answer to this question, in this particular instance.

"I'll take this one. The leash and the furry shrimp thing, too."

TEN

TUESDAY AFTERNOON WAS somewhat cloudy, but pleasantly mild, with a nice bit of wind to it. Evan had been cooped up in the office since just after sunrise, and he'd been relieved to get outside, where there always seemed to be more oxygen.

He and Goff had spent all morning talking to people with minor connections to or relationships with Bellamy and poring over his laptop and his financial records one more time. The laptop yielded very little. Downloaded copies of digital credit card statements, the last two years' tax returns, a lot of family photos, but no weird or threatening emails. Bellamy was barely active on Facebook and Instagram—his wife posted most of the statuses and just tagged him.

The pictures from their holiday vacation at Disney pissed Evan off. He was having a hard time finding some way that Bellamy had brought his demise upon himself, and the more he learned about him, the less optimistic he was that they'd find some reason that Bellamy had, if not deserved his murder, at least participated in the reason behind it. The idea that this had been some random, unprovoked thing would not only be depressing, it would also make the murderer harder to find.

Evan sat at the red light at Cecil B. Costen and Hwy 98, which would eventually become the main drag of Monument Avenue. Across the street, the bay sparkled at him, looking much more inviting than the lunch appointment to which he was dragging his feet. Along the bay was a park that Evan sometimes visited for free concerts in the salty humidity of summer evenings.

Evan turned right onto Hwy 98 and made his way to the very hip and beachy downtown area. It was comprised of several side streets housing small buildings from the thirties and upward, many of them with sharp new awnings, lots of potted flowers, and outdoor tables. The downtown area was a nice mix of restaurants, bars, antique places, and boutiques, and it reminded Evan a bit of downtown Cocoa. He liked it but often forgot to spend any time there.

He made a right on Second, then another on Reid, and pulled into a spot fairly close to the door of Provisions, a popular spot for happy hour, seafood and burgers. Evan had never been, but when James Quillen had suggested lunch at Dockside, Evan had countered with the first place that came to mind. He didn't like the idea of eating with the head of the county commissioners, his de facto boss, just yards from his own home. It might have been different if he liked Quillen, but he didn't.

Even with the brightness of the day muted somewhat by clouds, the interior of Provisions was an adjustment. It was full of dark wood and dim lighting. The place was crowded and a bit noisy, and it took a moment for him to see Quillen holding a hand up just to the right of the door. There were three booths there, and Quillen had commandeered the back one.

The man was all hale and hearty smiles, but he didn't bother to stand to greet Evan, just poked out a hand. Quillen was somewhere in his fifties, with dark hair barbered even more neatly than Evan's, and a salt and pepper beard that was so short it looked like makeup. His bright green eyes were the color of algae and no doubt enhanced by contacts.

Evan shook the man's hand and took a seat across from him. He noticed that Quillen already had a tall glass of iced tea in front of him.

"How are you, Evan?" Quillen asked.

"I'm fine, sir, thank you," Evan asked as he caught a server's eye. "And you?"

"Well, I'll be a whole lot happier when we've caught whoever's responsible for this…uh, incident."

"Won't we all?" Evan asked.

The server, a young guy with a bleached blond streak in his hair, approached the table, and Evan asked for his own sweet tea. Quillen advised he was on a tight schedule, so they went ahead and ordered. Evan got a small portion of the St. Joe Bouillabaisse. Quillen ordered a French Dip. Once Evan had his tea, Quillen leaned in for serious business.

"We need to be very proactive about this thing," he said, his voice lowered.

Evan felt that directing most of the SO's resources at investigating the case was pretty proactive. "How so?" he asked anyway.

"We can't let the press go off willy-nilly, making it sound worse than it is," Quillen answered.

"It would be a little difficult to make it sound better than it is," Evan said, trying not to sound irritated.

Quillen had foisted the sheriff's position onto Evan, no doubt because he thought this would make Evan his gofer. It was true, as Quillen had pointed out, that Evan needed the health insurance and the paycheck, but Evan had no desire to be the sheriff, now or in a year and a half when elections rolled around.

"You know what I'm saying," Quillen said, not bothering to hide *his* irritation. "We can't have the public thinking that someone's just going around stabbing people. No doubt, this guy, God rest him, probably got into something he shouldn't have or did something he shouldn't have to the wrong person."

"If he did, it's not immediately evident," Evan said. "So far, he's looking like an upstanding guy."

Quillen waved that thought away. "After the public debacle that Hutch put us through, we need the voters to know that we are on top of this, and every other crime in Gulf County."

"We are."

"But we need to look like it," Quillen said, which made little sense to Evan.

"All right," he said. "I'll make sure we look busier than we already are whenever the cameras are around."

He saw Quillen's nostrils flare just a bit. They were in an interesting position. Quillen was already figuring out that Evan wasn't going to be the lackey he was hoping for, but he'd look bad if he canned the guy that he himself had pushed for to take on the role of interim sheriff.

Evan had no doubt that Quillen had selfish reasons for putting him where he did, and he was also sure that Quillen had been trying to come up with some fresh ideas for making Evan more agreeable since a lack of ambition on Evan's part wasn't very useful. Evan wished him well, but he was never going to be Quillen's girlfriend.

The server came back with their food, and both men sat back and waited for him to leave.

"Where are we at with this situation, anyway?" Quillen asked after they were alone again.

"It's very early on," Evan answered. "But we have an entire team dedicated to the case, and it's our first priority."

"When do you think you'll make an arrest?"

Evan winced. Not only did it sound like a line from some TV cop show, but it was a stupid question. "I have no way of knowing that, Mr. Quillen."

Quillen tucked a corner of his sandwich into the dish of au jus, then let it drip a moment before taking a bite. He got a couple drops of beef juice on his lapel anyway, which made Evan curiously happy.

"Well, I need you to keep me abreast of everything that's going on," Quillen said, just before he was actually finished chewing. "I—we—want daily updates until this situation is resolved."

"I'll have Vi Hartigan send you daily reports," Evan said.

Quillen ate another hunk of his sandwich before setting it down and wiping his hands. "How's your poor wife doing?" he asked.

Quillen couldn't care less about Hannah, and Evan wondered if he was just trying to remind Evan of how much he needed his job.

"Her condition hasn't changed," Evan said to his soup. He didn't trust his ability to hide his distaste.

"She's been in that coma a long time, hasn't she?"

Evan took a spoonful of his soup. It was good, but he wasn't able to appreciate it, really, given the company. "Almost a year."

"That's got to be a hardship," Quillen said.

Evan didn't know if he meant financially, emotionally, or both, so he just nodded.

"Do they think there's a chance she'll recover?" Quillen said.

Evan bit back the first response that came to mind. The question was unkind, and why would they be keeping Hannah on the machines if there was no chance she'd awaken? Granted, the doctors had been pretty blunt about the odds.

"That's the hope," Evan said.

Quillen chewed for a moment, frowning thoughtfully into the space above Evan's head. "I hope the understandable stress of your situation doesn't interfere with your focus on the job," he said finally.

Evan took a sip of his tea before answering. "Actually, I think the opposite is true."

Evan was made to endure another thirty minutes of Quillen's company. Once he was back outside, watching Quillen's Lincoln pull out onto Reid, Evan lit up and took a long, grateful drag of his cigarette. He was distrustful of politicians in general, but he doubted Quillen's integrity more than most. At the very least, he disliked the man's attempts to put him in his place.

Evan had just slid into the Pilot when his cell phone rang. According to the screen, it was Vi.

"Hey, Vi," he answered.

There was just a moment's pause.

"This is Vi," she said, as he knew she would. "Mr. Nelson from Seminole Insurance called. He thinks he might have come across someone who had a serious issue with Jake Bellamy."

"Who is it?"

"He didn't say. I was at lunch when he called, otherwise I would have gotten the name."

"Okay, I'm just a few blocks away," Evan answered. "I'll stop by there. Anything else?"

"Nothing that won't wait until you get back," Vi answered.

"Oh, James Quillen would like you to send him daily reports. So that he knows we look like we're on top of things," he added dryly.

· ● ✳ ● ·

Evan waited fifteen minutes in the lobby of Seminole Insurance, while Nelson finished up with a client. He checked his messages, checked in with Goff, pretended to read a magazine on diabetes. The pregnant secretary offered him coffee, soda or bottled water, which he refused, politely, being careful to call her Llewellyn rather than Ginger. He was relieved when Nelson finally appeared, patting a large, sunburned man on the back and saying his goodbyes. He greeted Evan and led him back to his office. They both remained standing.

"So, I was going through Jake's client files like you asked, and I thought this might be relevant," he said, opening a manila folder. "Curt Wilkins. I remember Jake mentioning him, but it slipped my mind when you were here the other day."

"What about him?"

"Normally, he made the monthly premium payments on their life and auto insurance, but for whatever reason, his wife took over about a year ago. They were Phil's clients." He handed the file to Evan. "Anyway, she missed two payments, and their policies were canceled in December. Apparently, the wife didn't tell Wilkins. So, anyhow, his car was parked on the street downtown a few weeks ago, and some drunk hit it. Twice. The car was totaled."

"And he found out he didn't have insurance."

"Right," Nelson confirmed.

"But that's the wife's fault, not Bellamy's."

"I know, but when the guy called, he found out Jake was his new agent, and apparently he was really pissed and abusive on the phone. He called three times, actually. Jake came to me, and I told him there was nothing we could do, and he shouldn't worry about it, and to tell the guy to call me. He did, but I never heard from the man."

Evan looked at the copy of the man's driver's license in the auto insurance file. Slim, short of stature, with a hairline that started somewhere at the back of his head, apparently.

"Can you make me a copy of this?" Evan asked.

"Sure thing," Nelson answered. "You think it's anything?"

Evan shrugged. "It could be. We'll look into it."

Evan hadn't been optimistic about Curt Wilkins as a suspect, but he had been hopeful. As it turned out, that hope was wasted. Evan and Goff had gone to his marine supply store to talk to him and found that, although he was still pretty indignant about his policies being canceled, he had an excellent alibi. He'd been at a marine expo in Savannah that weekend.

They'd poke around at the idea that he might have hired someone to kill Bellamy, but Evan knew they were just fulfilling their due diligence; the guy just wasn't the type, and a hit would cost almost as much as replacing his car.

Evan had spent the rest of the afternoon continuing to run down acquaintances and going over Meyers' and Crenshaw's reports of same. Nothing remotely interesting came of it, and when Evan had gone to visit Hannah that evening, much of their one-sided conversation concerned the long shots of the widow and Phil Babcock. They didn't look likely, but they were better than nothing at all.

Evan had gone home, shared some take-out broiled snapper with Plutes, who hadn't thrown up on anything that day, and gone to bed no closer to figuring out who would have wanted to kill Jake Bellamy than he had been the morning he'd stood over the man's body.

It was almost one in the morning when Evan's cell phone jarred him out of a fitful sleep. It was Goff, calling from his own cell.

"Goff, what the hell?" Evan said by way of greeting.

"You're not kidding," Goff replied. "We got us another one."

"Another what?" Evan asked, though he already felt a sinking sensation in his gut.

"Another stabbing," Goff said. "Dispatch called Truman, Truman called me, and I'm out here calling you."

Evan sat up and rubbed at his hair to wake himself up. "Where are you?"

"Out at the Mainstay Suites next to the hospital," Goff answered. "Back parking lot."

"Give me ten minutes."

Evan hung up and hurried to his closet. He pulled down one of three identical pairs of navy trousers. Two pairs of the same trouser, in black, hung beside them. On the rod below, two suit blazers, one black, one navy, and four identical white shirts. Hannah used to tease him about his 'capsule wardrobe' as she called it, but it made getting dressed for work very easy, and he always knew when he needed to go to the dry cleaners.

He grabbed his holster from the nightstand and hurried up to the salon, stopping at a teak credenza to pick up his badge, wallet, and keys. Plutes, almost invisible in the dark, watched him from his spot under a portside window.

"I suppose its too much to ask for you to have some coffee waiting when I get back," Evan said.

Plutes agreed, silently, that it was.

ELEVEN

THE MAINSTAY WAS LOCATED on a stretch of 98 just outside town and was nestled between the sprawling Sacred Heart Hospital complex and the less sprawling Franklin/Gulf campus of Gulf Coast State College.

The hotel was set back from the road a good bit and surrounded by heavily-treed lots on either side and to the back. There weren't an awful lot of cars parked in the front lot, and the only reason there were more vehicles in back was that a whole lot of people were responding to a crime scene. Evan saw an ambulance with its lights off, three SO cruisers, Goff's small pickup, and one car from St. Joe PD. A small cluster of disheveled and worried-looking civilians stood just outside the back door.

As Evan was getting out of his vehicle, he saw the ME's van pulling in from the road. Goff, wearing tan slacks, blue disposable gloves, and a Carhartt jacket, spotted

DAWN LEE MCKENNA & AXEL BLACKWELL

him from where he stood next to an open Honda Civic at the back of the lot, and met Evan halfway there.

"What do we know?" Evan asked him.

"Tina Vicaro, twenty-four-year-old female, works as the second shift desk clerk," Goff said as they headed back the way he'd come. "She got off work at eleven, her relief said she left around ten minutes later. At twelve-thirty or so, feller over there named Marks came out here to his car to find his phone charger and saw her door open, went over there and found her."

"Where's he?"

Goff pointed about thirty feet away, where Deputy Means was talking to a man in his thirties wearing a red bathrobe and a pair of Crocs. "Means is talking to him. He's here with his wife, visiting her sister in the hospital."

"Okay, who else is here from the SO? I see Gordon," Evan said, nodding toward a deputy in his forties who was standing at the victim's car.

"Pauly's here," Goff answered as they reached the car.

Evan nodded at Deputy Means.

"Hey, boss," Means said.

"Gordon, do me a favor, grab the guy from PD and go get statements from those people staring at us," Evan said. "With any luck, somebody saw or heard something."

"Will do," Gordon said, stepping back from the car's open driver side door.

On the asphalt beyond him, a few feet back from the door was the body of Tina Vicaro.

She was slim, very pretty, and well-tanned, with long, light brown hair pulled into a ponytail. Her blonde highlights shone under the light of the vehicles parked around her. She was wearing a light blue button-down shirt with a nametag, but there wasn't a lot of blue left to it. Most of the front of her shirt, from her right breast to the waist of her khaki pants, was blood-soaked.

Evan squatted down, his nose twitching at the coppery, almost humid air around the girl. He counted at least five cuts in the shirt, most of them in the upper right chest. He looked up as Goff squatted down next to him.

"She's just a little tyke," Goff said, his eyes solemn.

"Yeah."

"Looks like Nick Stapleton's here for the ME."

Evan looked over his shoulder as a slightly round young man with wire-rimmed glasses and wispy blond hair hurried their way with his kit in his hand. Evan had only met the guy once before when he'd come to collect a drowning victim from Cape San Blas. He didn't know enough to have an opinion of him.

"Second stabbing death in a week," Evan said to Goff. "You'd think Grundy would kind of be anxious to show up for that, if for nothing else, then for the press attention."

"I keep waiting for you to figure out that the only thing Grundy's gonna do for you is sign off on other people's work," Goff said.

"I think I'm picking up on it," Evan said. Stapleton stopped a few feet away, and Evan looked over his shoulder at him. "Thanks for coming, Stapleton, but we're not ready for you, yet." He looked at Goff. "Trigg coming?"

"She's a few minutes out yet, but she's *en route.*"

"Just hang out for a bit, Nick, okay?" Evan said.

"Yeah, sure," Nick said. He headed back to his van at a relaxed lope.

Evan looked back down at the body of Tina Vicaro. "Is she local?"

"Local license," Goff said, "but I don't know her, or any other Vicaros."

"Okay." Evan stood up and leaned over to look inside the car.

An Android phone, a pair of white earbuds, and an open Snickers bar sprawled across the passenger seat, but the girl's purse, one of those paisley fabric things, lay on the ground near the back tire on the driver's side.

"Looks like maybe she had started to get in, or was in when he hit. No blood inside, so he either grabbed her right before she got in or he pulled her out before he started stabbing her."

"You'd think she'd have a second to scream then," Goff said.

"We don't know that she didn't," Evan said. "Not yet, anyway."

He stood up, pulled a pair of disposable gloves from his back pocket, and looked over at the group of onlookers. "Do me a favor, get a few more guys out here. I want anyone, guests or staff, who's not already out here to be spoken to. Maybe somebody saw someone hanging around back here earlier, or saw something else we can use. Where's the night clerk?"

"She went back inside," Goff said. "She said she needed to get back to the desk, but I think she was just pretty freaked out. I told her not to contact anyone about this yet."

"Okay. Go inside, let her know we can't let anyone check out until we've spoken to all of the guests here. We also can't have anyone checking in, or anyone else clocking out, janitors, maintenance, whomever."

"Gotcha," Goff said and straightened up. "Here comes Trigg."

Goff headed for the hotel, and Evan turned to watch Trigg make her way to him, kit in hand. She was wearing her SO polo, but it was wrinkled like she might have slept in it. Her bobbed hair was pulled up in a clip.

"Hey," she said, without much enthusiasm.

"Hey, Trigg," Evan said. "We wake you up?"

"No, I was binge-watching *A Full House*." At Evan's quizzical expression, she rolled her eyes. "Of course, you woke me up. What am I, a vampire?"

She set down her kit and pulled out a pair of gloves. "I grabbed Pauly and asked him to tape it off," she said.

"Okay," Evan replied. Over her shoulder, he saw Paulsen stretching yellow tape between a non-working light pole and a small bush planted in a median. "Need to find out how long that light's been out."

The next closest one was almost to the front door. If the light had been out when she got here, the girl should have parked closer to the door. He wanted to go back a few hours and tell her that.

"Look at these scratches on her face," Trigg was saying.

Evan squatted down next to her. There were two scratches near her mouth, just barely visible, on the side of her face that had been turned toward the ground. There were a couple of minute drops of blood on one of them.

The girl's eyes were open and were already starting to cloud over. They'd been a pretty brown.

"Go ahead and get your pictures of the interior of the car," Evan said. "I want to take a look at her phone."

Evan stood up and stood aside as Trigg pulled out her camera and started taking shots of the front seat. A couple of minutes later, Goff and Means hurried up to him.

"Means might have something," Goff said.

Means looked down at a small notepad. "The guy over there in the Hurricanes jersey," he said. "He came out for a smoke maybe eleven-fifteen, eleven-thirty, he's not sure. He had just lit up and was checking his Facebook when he heard some guy raise his voice, but when he looked up, he didn't see anything."

"Did he hear what the guy said?"

"Yeah, he said it was 'You can't have it, either' or something really close to that. He's wigged out now, so he's not sure, but he said he thinks that's what it was. He said it sounded angry, but not scary or anything, and he didn't see anybody or hear anything else, so he figured maybe he was hearing something from over by the pool or one of the rooms."

"But it was a male voice?"

"Yeah, that he's sure of."

"Anybody over there that saw or talked to this girl tonight?"

"Yeah, lady from Tampa, on her way home from Pensacola," he said. "She checked in around seven and the girl took care of her. She says she was really sweet, very upbeat, seemed in a good mood."

"Okay, go back and help get the rest of their statements, then help with interviewing the guests inside. Goff, we got some people on the way for that?"

"Yeah, we got another couple guys from PD coming. There's a cruiser out front blocking the entrance now, too."

"Ok, thanks," Evan said. "Thanks, Means," he said as the deputy headed back to the cluster of onlookers.

"Hey, Evan, you can take a look at her phone now," Trigg said behind him.

He walked back over to the car, opened it from the passenger side. Goff was right behind him. He picked up the phone and tapped it. The screen lit up, and he pressed the Home button, grateful that it was an Android and not an iPhone. If need be, Androids were easier to break into.

Fortunately, Tina Vicaro didn't seem too concerned about her privacy; the phone wasn't password protected. He thumbed his way to her contacts list.

"Whatcha hoping for?" Goff said.

"Jake Bellamy," Evan answered. "Maybe we just found out why someone hated him enough to kill him."

It was close to four in the morning by the time the body had been processed, the scene had been gone over with a fine-toothed comb, and everyone on the property had been interviewed. Evan had kept the evidence bags holding Tina Vicaro's cell phone, keys, and wallet, and they sat on the passenger seat as he followed Goff to Tina's address on Garrison Avenue.

The address turned out to be a small house of CBS construction, that looked like a million other houses built in Florida in the sixties and seventies. It was neatly kept, though, and in the light that shone from a fixture by the front door, Evan could see several pots of flowers and tropical plants. A green Volkswagen, one of the new bugs but not itself new, sat in the driveway. There was no garage.

He and Goff closed their doors quietly, though Evan couldn't have said why; they were about to wake up anyone who was inside anyway. He waited a moment for Goff to reach him, then they walked up the path of

Chattahoochee rock, their shoes crunching loudly in the quiet night. There was no porch, just a small concrete stoop. Evan went up the two steps and knocked on the door, louder than he normally would have.

As he waited for someone to answer, he looked around him. Next to the steps, underneath a hibiscus, a pottery rabbit stared at nothing in particular. A black metal mailbox hung by the door, boasting a Ron Jon's Surf Shop bumper sticker. It was faded and torn and looked like someone had tried to peel it off at some point.

When there was no sound of anyone coming after thirty seconds, Evan knocked again, a little more loudly. About ten seconds later, a light went on beyond the front door, maybe a hallway. A moment after that, a woman's voice called through the door.

"Who is it?"

"Ma'am, this is the Gulf County Sheriff's Office. We need to speak with you, please."

Evan pulled out his badge and held it up in front of the peephole. After a long moment, the door opened, but with the chain still on. A pale forehead and one green eye peered around the door.

"You're not in uniform," the woman said. Her voice was shaky.

"No, ma'am, I'm sorry, we're not. I'm Sheriff Evan Caldwell, and this is Sgt. Ruben Goff."

Goff held up his own badge and the eyeball looked past Evan to inspect it, though there was no way she could have read it.

"Those aren't Sheriff's cars."

"I understand and respect your caution, ma'am. If you'd feel more comfortable, we'll wait here while you call the Sheriff's Office and verify our identities. They know we're here."

The eye bounced between him and Goff for a moment, then Evan heard the chain slide and the door opened. The woman standing there was no more than twenty-five, with white blonde hair and a high forehead. She was wearing yoga pants and a hoodie.

"What's going on?" the girl asked.

"Can I ask your name, miss?" Evan asked gently.

"Carrie Winters," she answered, barely above a whisper. Nobody expected good news when a cop knocked on their door at four in the morning.

"Ms. Winters, may we come in?"

She thought about it a second. "I'm sorry, but you're making me really nervous. Maybe I should call."

"Carrie, does Tina Vicaro live here?" Evan asked quickly.

"Tina?" Her eyes darted to the driveway. "Where's her car? Has she been in an accident?"

"No, but she has been hurt," Evan answered. "Why don't you go call my office? We really should talk inside."

She blinked at him a few times, then opened the door wider. "No, come in."

She backed up to let them inside, and Goff gently closed the door behind them.

"Ma'am," he said with a nod.

"Is there somewhere we can sit down?" Evan asked.

She opened her mouth to answer, then seemed to forget what she was about to say. She nodded instead and led them through into a formal dining room to the right. She flicked on the light, then sat down at the head of the table. Evan and Goff took two seats on the near side.

"What's happened?" Carrie asked.

"Is Tina your sister?"

"My roommate," she answered, her eyes wide, pupils constricted. "We know each other from high school."

"Is there someone else here with you?" Evan asked, though he was sure they'd be standing there if there were.

"No. My mom…this is my mom's house, but she got married…she lives in Vero now."

"I see." Evan rubbed at his scar. "And does Tina work at Mainstay Suites?"

"Yes." Her eyes flicked from Evan to Goff and back again.

Evan pulled out his phone. He'd taken a picture of Tina's driver's license. "Is this Tina?"

The girl's nostrils flared, and her lower lip shook. "Yes." Evan barely heard her.

"I'm sorry, Carrie, but Tina was attacked and killed as she was leaving work tonight."

Evan waited. Some people erupted immediately, with tears, rage or both. Others had to let it seep into them, like water into carpet. Carrie was the latter. She blinked several times, though her eyes didn't tear up, but she had gone a shade paler in the last thirty seconds.

"I don't understand," she said finally. "Why?"

"We don't know that yet," Evan answered. "Has anyone bothered her lately? Anyone made her worry a little?"

Carrie shook her head. Her pale hair was coming out of its bun, and a tendril of it fell from her forehead. "No. No, nothing like that."

"Does she have a boyfriend?"

"Yeah, sure," Carrie answered, nodding. "Michael."

"What's Michael's last name?' Evan asked, as he heard Goff's pen scratching beside him.

"Pittfield," she answered. "But they're doing great. I mean, great. They're getting…planning on getting married." Evan saw her hands start to shake as she lifted them to her face, but she didn't cry.

"What about family? Does she have family here?" he asked her.

Carrie took her hands down and stared at the table. "Her mom passed away three years ago. Breast cancer. She doesn't have a relationship with her father. But, um, she has an aunt. In Pensacola."

"We'll need to know how to get in touch with her, just in case she's not in Tina's phone contacts."

"She is, but I have it, too," Carrie said. She rubbed at her face like she was chasing away the last cobwebs of sleep. "Okay, wait. What actually happened? What happened to her?"

"It looks like she was attacked as she was getting into her car," Evan said. "She was stabbed."

Carrie covered her mouth, and tears appeared suddenly and slid down her cheeks. "Oh my—oh, Tina." She shook her head and swiped at the tears. "Did you catch the guy?"

"Not yet," Evan said quietly.

"Well, I mean—did somebody see it happen? Do you know who did it?"

"No," Evan said. "We do have some witnesses who might have heard something, but the camera by the back door was disabled."

"Wait!" she exclaimed. "There was something, but it, well it ended up being nothing."

"What's that?" Evan asked.

"Well, she lost her wallet," Carrie answered. "This was…maybe a week and a half ago? She had to cancel all her cards, get a new license, everything. And then a few days later, she found it in her trunk. Her trunk's a mess, you know, all kinds of beach gear and her gym stuff and everything. It was in there. But I guess somebody could have stolen it and put it back, right? No, that doesn't actually make sense. I'm sorry."

"It's okay. Everything is worth looking at," Evan told her. "We want to make sure that whoever did this to her is punished."

The girl nodded at a space beyond Evan, maybe beyond the room.

"Carrie, do you know a man by the name of Jake Bellamy?" Evan asked.

She thought about it a moment, then shook her head. "No."

"Do you remember Tina ever mentioning the name, or someone named Jake?"

"No. Why? Do you think he's the one who hurt her?"

"No, but we're looking at a few different things."

"I don't understand," she said, her voice rising an octave. "Who is he?"

"He's someone else who was hurt recently," Evan said vaguely. "I'm sorry, but it's not something we can really go into at the moment."

She looked like she was about to ask again, but she stopped, mouth open, and then seemed to shift her focus.

"Where is she? Somebody should be with her!"

Carrie moved as though to stand, and Evan put a hand on her shoulder, but just barely.

"Our people are with her right now. We're taking care of her, I promise," Evan assured her. "Ma'am, do you have someplace you can go, where someone can be with you?"

She looked alarmed. "Do you think he'd come here?"

"It's unlikely, ma'am. But you've just had a big shock and you shouldn't be here alone."

"We're also going to need to take a look at her room, her things," Evan added. "You can stay here for that if you're more comfortable, but it might be easier for you if you didn't."

Carrie's eyes darted around the room for a few seconds. "I can go to my sister's house. She and her husband live in Apalach."

"Would you like to call her?' Evan asked. "Then if you want, we can have someone follow you there. For your own peace of mind."

"Okay. I guess." She looked around the room. "I need to…I need to take some stuff for work. I go in at seven, and I'm not sure I'll be able to call out."

"Where do you work?"

"The hospital," she answered. "I'm a NICU nurse."

"Would you like me to call someone, your supervisor?" Evan asked her.

She shook her head. "No, I'll do it. They'll let me call out if they can. It's just that we're shorthanded."

Evan nodded. "Okay."

He waited as Carrie stared at her hands, folded in front of her on the table. He gave her a minute to say whatever she was thinking to say.

She didn't look at him when she finally spoke. "Did she suffer? Do you think she had time to be scared?"

Evan saw a tear drip onto the back of her hand.

"I think it was over very quickly," he answered, and hoped that it was mostly true.

Half an hour later, Carrie had packed an overnight bag. Evan watched her back out of her driveway and head toward 98, an SO cruiser behind her. She'd held it together really well, and Evan imagined she was probably a pretty good nurse to have around in a crisis.

She'd shown Evan which of Tina Vicaro's keys went to the front door of the house, then shown him to her room. Then she was gone, leaving Evan and Goff, standing like home invaders in the center of a dead girl's room.

"I could get by on my pension 'til my social security kicks in," Goff said quietly, picking up a stuffed elephant from Tina's nightstand.

"I thought you didn't want to retire," Evan said half-heartedly.

"Some days I do." Goff put the stuffed animal down.

The room, like the rest of the house, was simply furnished with mostly older furniture, but it was clean and cheerful and almost offensive in light of what had happened to its occupant. Every time he came to a scene like this, Evan always wondered if the person had had some inkling, something, even an unexplained goosebump, that hinted they would never be back. It amazed him, really, that most often, people were oblivious to their own mortality, their own bad luck, right up until they were looking straight at it. He supposed it was a blessing, but sometimes, when he thought about it, it made him nervous.

It took Evan and Goff less than forty minutes to collect Tina's laptop, her iPad, a notebook that was half-journal, half-drawing pad, several bank and credit card statements, and a small recent-looking photo album, the kind that drugstores and online places put together.

Evan locked the door behind them as they left. The sky was just turning pink, and there was a light breeze coming from the west. It was going to be a beautiful day.

TWELVE

BEFORE HEADING TO THE SO, Evan had stopped by his boat for a quick shower, shave, and coffee. A violent murder in a quiet town like Port St. Joe strained the resources of any law enforcement community under the best circumstances, but a second murder compounded those demands exponentially.

In the public's eyes, a second murder, especially one as seemingly random as this, suggested the possibility of an imminent third murder, and a fourth. It was no longer good enough just to solve the case, Evan and his team had to solve it quickly, and Evan felt the pressure of it almost physically, like the building of a good swell behind him. He knew cops who, under the gun on a case, did better by going without sleep, decent food, or a break. Evan responded in the opposite way; he needed order, routine, and certain physical standards in order to think more clearly.

Goff had headed straight to the SO with all the materials he and Evan had collected at Tina Vicaro's home. Sgt. Peters was manning the station, working on the end of shift report.

Barely two hours after leaving Tina Vicaro's home, Evan had assembled a dozen deputies and PSJ Police officers in the SO's small conference room. Goff had been busy collecting and organizing photos of their two victims as well as anyone closely associated with either. These he had pinned to the large corkboard on the wall. He had grouped the pictures to indicate which persons were associated with which victims.

The Bellamy murder had dominated the headlines since Saturday, so everyone in the room already knew his face well. Evan wanted the task force, which had doubled in number overnight, to be equally familiar with every other face connected to their investigation. PSJ's population was small enough and friendly enough, that it would be almost impossible for any individual in town to go unrecognized by at least one deputy or officer in a room full of them. It was Evan's hope that his team's familiarity with the local faces would help connect the two victims in ways that he as an outsider might miss, no matter how focused he tried to be.

He started to present a quick rundown of the new murder for the officers and deputies who had not been to the crime scene. Halfway through the details they were able to get from the scene, Evan noticed two officers visibly shaken by the news of Tina Vicaro's murder. One PSJ officer coughed loudly, though the cough was obviously a cover for some less-manly noise, then excused himself and disappeared into the hall.

Evan watched him go, and suddenly felt guilty for not notifying the officers of the victim's identity before placing them all in a room with her picture tacked to the wall at the center of a murder investigation. In his haste to get on top of the case, Evan hadn't considered that any of his deputies, or the PSJ officers, might actually be close to the new victim.

It took Evan only half a second to realize he had stopped talking. Before anyone else noticed, Goff stepped in and completed the case summary. "We can't say for certain that one case has got anything to do with the other, but it don't take a federal agent to figure they're connected. We've got similar looking knife wounds. We won't know for sure until the ME, or someone who actually *works* at the ME's office, has a look at it, but we're guessing same man, same knife."

Goff rubbed at his mustache, smoothing down the silver-dusted whiskers, then looked back up at the room.

"Both attacks were brutal, violent, out in the open. No attempt to hide the body, no obvious robbery. Neither victim seems the type to make enemies, but somebody was madder than hell and took it out on them." He motioned to the photos on the wall. "We've got to figure out why. We've got to figure out what connects these two."

"What if nothing connects them?" a voice called from the back of the room. "What if it's just some random slasher?" It was a young guy from PD.

Evan saw the corner of Goff's jaw tighten. Nobody wanted the focus to go in that direction. He answered for Goff. "That would be a much less likely scenario. The timing and location of these attacks suggest the killer intentionally targeted these two victims." Evan paused, then added, "The violence of the attacks leads me to believe he has a lot of rage. That type of rage feeds on itself, feeds on violence. Whoever did this was angry with these two people specifically."

Evan let his words settle, then turned and nodded to Goff. Goff hefted a stack of hastily stuffed manila folders.

"Pass these around; everybody take one.," Goff said. "I've been running since before the rooster and haven't even had a chance to straighten my shorts yet, so don't expect those files to be in any sort of order, but everything you'll need is in there. I got guest records and an employee list from the hotel, phone records from about ten different phones, Jake's client list, Tina's Face Plant friends, Jake's coworkers, Tina's coworkers…just about every possible way these two could have crossed paths. Each folder has an assignment. Somebody's gonna get the video from the hotel, somebody's gonna get phone numbers to cross-reference. Don't be choosy, just take whichever lands in your lap, and get to work."

"Please, though," Evan interjected, "do let Vi know which assignment you pulled."

Goff nodded at him, then turned back to the crew. "Be thorough but do it quick-like. We don't have room on this wall for too many more photos."

· ● ✴ ● ·

Evan didn't want to go back to the Bellamy home. Telling someone their loved one was dead, and became so violently, was bad enough. Going back to ask uncomfortable questions about that loved one seemed worse, at least to Evan.

He had called ahead, and Karen Bellamy had apparently been watching out the living room window for him. She was standing at the front door when he parked at the curb. The driveway held three cars in addition to those that belonged to the Bellamys.

She stepped back and made room for him to come inside. Evan noticed that she looked ten years older than she had just a few days before. New lines circled her eyes and etched her forehead. The shadows beneath her eyes testified to a lack of sleep.

Evan heard several voices, adults and children, coming from the back of the house as Karen led him into the living room. Karen noticed him noticing.

"My mom and sister are here, and Jake's brother and sister-in-law." She gestured for Evan to sit in the same chair he'd occupied on his first visit to the home.

Evan sat and leaned forward, his elbows on his knees. "Would you like one of them to come in here with you?"

She sat down, knees together, hands folded tightly in her lap. "Do I need them to? I mean, should I?"

"That's up to you, Karen. I'm just suggesting it in case you'd be more comfortable, but I do have some sensitive questions to ask you," he said. "Just so you know."

She thought about it for just a few seconds. "I think I'd prefer to talk alone."

"Okay." Evan pulled out his notebook. "Karen, do you know a woman named Tina Vicaro?"

She seemed startled by the question, and she gave it some thought. "No, I don't think so."

He pulled out his phone, with the picture of Tina's driver's license. "Do you recognize this woman? Have you seen her anywhere?"

Karen took his phone and studied the picture. Evan guiltily saw the shadow pass over her face, saw her notice how young and how pretty Tina Vicaro had been.

She shook her head finally. "No, I'm almost positive." She handed the phone back to Evan. "Why? Who is she?"

"She was attacked and killed leaving her work last night," Evan answered quietly.

"The same as Jake?"

"Pretty much, yes," Evan answered. "Did you and your husband ever stay at the Mainstay Suites over by the hospital? Maybe when you were visiting or looking for a new home?"

She was shaking her head before he finished. "No. We came every weekend for almost a month when we were looking for this house, but we had a vacation rental. The company paid for it."

Evan made a note, though he really didn't need to. "Did your husband ever come here alone? Maybe for an interview with Seminole?"

"No. We came with him."

"And you stayed at the vacation rental that time?"

"Yes," she answered. Her hands twisted in her lap. "Can you—why are you asking?"

"Well, Port St. Joe isn't exactly a hotbed of murder, or violent crime, for that matter," he answered. "Now we have two murders, with a number of similarities, so we have to assume it's likely there's some connection."

"Between the victims, you mean." Her voice had gone flat.

"Yes."

Karen Bellamy took a long, even breath, then let it out slowly. "Well, she might belong to our church, I don't know. Or be a client. But I don't know her personally." She sat up a bit straighter. "And I don't think Jake did, either."

"Karen, understand that I'm not implying there was anything untoward going on, or that Jake was doing anything wrong at all," Evan said gently. "They might have gone to the same gym, or they might even both know the attacker without knowing each other. But there's almost certainly something that ties them together."

That wasn't completely true; the most likely connection was some kind of relationship, and either someone in Jake's life objecting, or someone in Tina's. However, that wasn't a fact, as yet, and Evan didn't like the idea that he might well be planting a hurtful untruth in her mind.

"Sheriff Caldwell," she said after a moment. "I know fidelity isn't very popular, and I'm sure you see a lot of cheating spouses in your line of work. But Jake and I were best friends as well as a couple. I knew his character."

"I understand," Evan replied quietly. "Please understand that these are questions I have to ask."

After a moment, she nodded.

"Karen, did your husband have a computer at home?"

"He has a laptop."

"I'd like to borrow it for a couple of days. We might be able to find something there that will tell us why he was targeted."

"Like what?"

Evan shook his head. "We don't know. An argument with someone in an online group, an email that seems threatening or angry; we won't know until we see it. If we see anything."

"Okay," she said, but he knew she was offended.

She stood up. "It's in the den. I'll go get it."

Evan stood and remained standing after she'd gone. He tucked his notebook and pen back in his blazer pocket, then turned around and found himself facing a small console table. On top were several framed photos of Jake Bellamy. His wife and kids were in all of them. Evan had to admit the man looked content to be where he was in those pictures. Evan had noticed sometimes, that a subject was wearing a big smile in a picture, but their eyes looked like their mind was somewhere else. He didn't see that in Jake Bellamy's photographs, and while the lack of a relationship between Bellamy and Tina Vicaro would make his job harder, he hoped, for Karen Bellamy's sake, that he didn't find one.

"Here you go," Karen said behind him.

She held out a modest, black 17-inch HP. Its power cable was looped in a bundle on top. Evan took it from her.

"The password is 'Bahamababy2002,'" she said. She gave him a small smile. "Our honeymoon. He wasn't exactly secretive."

Evan nodded, almost apologetically he hoped. "Thank you."

He tucked the laptop under one arm and held out a hand. She took it, and her grip was firm without making a point. "Thank you, Karen. I'll let you know as soon as we know anything important."

"Thank you."

She preceded Evan to the door and let him out. It had gotten back up into the forties or fifties, and he took in a great lungful of the fresh air, relieved to be back outside, away from Karen Bellamy's pain and any part he was playing in it.

When he got to his vehicle, she was still in the doorway, staring at something across the street. When he looked, he saw a couple in their sixties or seventies, in the driveway of a neat, ranch-style home. The husband was putting two overnight bags in the trunk of a late-model Toyota sedan, and the wife was slapping him on the shoulder. They were both laughing.

When Evan turned back to the front door, Karen Bellamy was gone.

He got back to the SO at just past noon. He checked Tina Vicaro's laptop and both victims' cell phones out of evidence and carried them and Bellamy's laptop with him as he entered Vi's office. Vi was out to lunch, apparently. He closed his office door behind him, set the laptops and phone on his desk, and set aside his paper files before sitting down in his chair.

He pulled out his cell and called Goff. Goff answered on the first ring.

"Goff," he said.

"Goff, where are you right now?"

"My desk."

"Could you come to my office for a few minutes? I've got something for you."

"Is it lunch, or should I bring mine with me?"

"It's not lunch. Feel free to bring yours."

A couple of minutes later, Goff gave one knock and then walked into the office. He held a legal pad in one hand and an old-fashioned lunch box in the other, one of those with the domed lid that held a metal thermos.

"Hey, Goff, have a seat," Evan said, opening the plastic envelope that contained Tina Vicaro's laptop. "Just move those files over so you have room to eat."

"I'm almost afraid to eat in here, clean as this desk is," Goff said, sitting down.

"I eat in here all the time," Evan said.

"Yeah, but you eat like an elderly British lady," Goff countered.

"What do you mean?"

"If you've ever dripped Miracle Whip anywhere, I wasn't there to see it."

Evan tossed him a look. Goff ignored it, flipping the clasp on his lunch box. He took out the metal thermos, then smiled at his lunch.

"My bride takes good care of me," Goff said. "Never the same thing twice in a row." He unscrewed the cap on his Thermos, and a fragrant steam crept out of it. "Nothing for a cold day like tomato soup and a tuna fish sandwich." He looked up at Evan. "Ya eat yet? There's plenty."

Evan couldn't help smiling. He'd never met anyone more comfortable in his own skin. "No, thanks, you go ahead," Evan answered. "I grabbed something on the way back," he fibbed.

Goff unfolded a paper placemat with a Christmas tree design and placed a low, square piece of Tupperware on it. Then he pulled out a matching napkin and stuck it into his collar. Once it was situated, he took out a small piece of notepaper, unfolded it, and smiled as he read a few words. Then he bowed his head for just a second before opening the container. The sandwich was wrapped in wax paper, with a couple of pieces of iceberg lettuce on the outside. Goff tucked them into his sandwich and took a bite.

"How long have you been married, Goff?" Evan asked.

Goff chewed and swallowed before answering. "Gonna be forty years in July. Got married right outa high school."

"That's impressive."

"Nothing to it," Goff answered. "Long as you're married to my wife."

Evan had met Goff's wife once. She wasn't five feet tall, and she was even skinnier than Goff. She wore her long, graying red hair in a frizzy braid that hung down her bony back and not an ounce of makeup, but he'd seen Goff watching her like she was a supermodel. It was at that moment that Evan had decided Goff might be one of the better men he'd ever met.

"So, what have you got for me?" Goff asked.

"I got Bellamy's laptop from his wife," Evan said. "She doesn't have any idea who Tina Vicaro is, and she's pretty convincing in her belief that Bellamy didn't know her, either. But there's got to be a connection somewhere, even if it's innocent."

"Okay," Goff said, polishing off the first half of his sandwich.

"I'm going to go through their laptops, try to find some communication between them, or barring that, shared Facebook friends, common online groups, something. I'll also look through her stuff to see what I can find out about her boyfriend and their relationship. Any luck with him?"

"Yep. Caught him at work," Goff answered. "He works over at the electric company. Says he was home in bed when Tina was killed. Nobody to corroborate, so we'll have to keep looking at him. Seems like a decent sort, although I've been wrong before."

"How'd he seem about Tina's death?"

"Pretty genuinely wrecked." Goff took a sip of his soup. The bottom of his mustache came back trimmed in red. "But like I said, I've been fooled before."

"Where are you going next with him?"

"Got an appointment at two to talk to her aunt, see what she knows about their relationship. She got in from Pensacola little bit ago, but she's going to the morgue. Insisted. I offered to go with her, but she said no."

Evan nodded. "Okay. Meyers and Crenshaw still talking to her contacts?"

"Yep. So far, nothing. Nobody saying she had any problems with anybody, and nobody saying she had any relationship trouble, either." Goff wiped at his mouth. "Oh, hey. Paula called while you were gone. DNA from the hair on Bellamy? Not in the system."

"Figures," Evan said.

All that meant was that he hadn't been in the military, at least not recently, nor had his DNA been collected as evidence in another case. It would have been really nice if the database had yakked out a name for them, but Evan's luck didn't run that way, so he hadn't been expecting it.

"Okay. Do me a favor," Evan said. "Give Meyers and Crenshaw the cell phones. I know neither Tina nor Bellamy had each other in their contacts or recent calls, but let's see if they have any overlapping contacts. I don't care if it's their hairdresser. There's a string in between these two people, even if they never heard of each other."

Goff pulled the evidence bags containing the cell phones over to his side of the desk. "Will do." He took another drink of his soup and watched Evan stare at the wall, tapping his pen against the desk.

"So, we know what we know, and we know what we don't know, and there's a whole lot more of that," Goff said. "But what do you *think*?"

Evan considered his answer for a moment. "I think if we don't find the connection between these two people, no matter how small, we have no chance in hell of finding out who killed them. We don't have enough evidence. No witnesses, other than the hotel guest who heard something and saw nothing."

"What if there is no connection?" Goff asked.

"Then our problem gets a whole lot worse," Evan said.

THIRTEEN

ONCE GOFF HAD TAKEN his lunchbox and his leave, Evan buried himself in the electronic comings and goings of Jake Bellamy and Tina Vicaro. The task at hand was necessarily laborious. Without some IT genius available to run that data from both computers to look for commonalities, Evan was forced to pull up Jake's email and search for emails from Tina's, then pull up Tina's and search for emails to or from Jake, just in case one of them knew how to scrub their emails better than the other. It took almost two hours to find out that, unless they had email accounts that weren't showing up in their histories, neither of them had ever emailed the other.

Evan then moved on to searching through both email accounts to see if any weird, mean, or otherwise suspicious emails had been sent or received. Evan was done with Jake, who had dumped his email more regularly, within an hour, and had just started on Tina's when his intercom buzzed at him.

"Yes, Vi," he answered tiredly.

"This is Vi," came the reply. "Danny Coyle is on line three for you."

"Thank you," Evan said and switched buttons. "Hey, Danny."

"Oh, hey!" Danny exclaimed, like Evan had unexpectedly called him. "So, I slaved away, and I have your autopsy report in hand. Do you want me to email it, tell you over the phone and then email it or do you want to hear it in person?"

"I take it you've finally been granted permission to transmit reports via email."

"Oh, yeah, no. But I figured out Grundy's password," Danny said. "Rumrunner II. It's the name of his boat."

"Grundy has a boating license?"

"Scary, I know," Danny replied. Evan could almost feel him nodding. "So, email?"

"Yes, but I'll be there in a few minutes anyway."

When Evan walked into the autopsy lab, it was empty, save for the body of Tina Vicaro and whoever was loitering in the stainless-steel body drawers, of which there was a bank of eight. He walked over to the table where Tina Vicaro was lying, her body covered head to toe in the thick, opaque plastic sheeting that made every body look sinister.

He glanced over at the granite counter beside him, grabbed a pair of gloves from an open box, and pulled them on. Then he pulled the sheeting back, uncovered Tina's face, and folded the plastic over her chest.

It always surprised Evan how rapidly any signs of life disappeared from the physical body. The night before, Tina's skin had been richly tanned, though not terribly dark, and her hair had been shiny and sleek.

Today, Evan looked down at a face that was gray and drawn, the skin looser and as dry as a lizard's. Her hair had lost its luster overnight and looked stiff and unhealthy. She had been a pretty girl, pretty enough that it would still be apparent even if he'd not been to the scene. Evan had only glanced at her photo album before he'd bagged it, but Tina Vicaro had had an open, welcoming smile, one that said she didn't expect anything hurtful and terrible to be headed her way. It made him sad, but he'd been sad when he got there.

"Oh, hey!" Danny said behind him.

Evan looked over his shoulder as Danny let the door to the back of the lab, whatever that contained, fall slowly closed.

"Hey, Danny," Evan said. "Just having a look. Hope you don't mind."

"No, no, I know you know what you're about, right?" Danny pulled on his own gloves and stood on the other side of the table. He looked down at Tina's face, his expression somber. "Sad, seriously. The whole time I was working on her, I couldn't help thinking that if I'd met her out there somewhere, you know, like The Pig or 7-11 or something, she would have been one of those girls that made me really anxious."

"What do you mean?"

"You know, nerves. Social dysfunction and whatnot," Danny said. He looked back down at Tina. "But I would have wanted to at least say 'hi.'"

Evan didn't know what to say to that. He wasn't sure if he was touched or uncomfortable. "She was a pretty girl," he said, just for something to say.

Danny heaved out a big sigh. "Yep, she was." Then he looked up at Evan, his face suddenly animated. "So, autopsy, though! Very interesting!"

"How so?"

"Well, first of all, and I don't know if you were expecting this or if it's going to kill your day, but the knife that killed this girl is the same one that killed Jacob Bellamy."

"Given the low rate of stabbing deaths in Port St. Joe, I pretty much expected that."

"Yeah, I figured. Anyhoodles, same knife. I compared the slides meticulously."

"I believe you."

"Now for some dissimilarities."

Danny pulled the sheet down to Tina Vicaro's hips. Evan felt bad, wanted to cover her small breasts for her.

"Okay, so, first things first," Danny said. "There are fewer stab wounds, though they're all concentrated in pretty much the same area as with Jacob, in the upper right quadrant. Five wounds. Two punctured the liver, one the right lung, and the other two missed vital organs. However, one of those nicked the lateral thoracic artery pretty thoroughly. That was most likely the wound that killed her, though the others would have killed her shortly thereafter anyway."

He looked up at Evan apologetically.

"It's difficult to nail down when death is so quick and all of the wounds would have caused enough blood loss, right, but I think that one was probably either the final wound, or one administered seconds after her heart stopped beating. I saw the pictures of the scene, and there wasn't as much blood as you'd see if that had been the first or even second wound. You know, arterial. Bad."

Evan sighed and rubbed a hand over his face. Every now and then, it occurred to him that his choice of occupation wasn't really all that normal. What kind of people were he and Danny and Goff and Trigg, to choose to deal so closely with violent death?

"Okay," Danny went on. "So, another variance. This attack was from behind."

Evan looked up at him. "Are you sure?"

"Oh, sure, yeah," Danny said. "The angle of the wounds is markedly upward, but the attacker is at least six feet, probably six one or two. In order to achieve this tra-

DAWN LEE MCKENNA & AXEL BLACKWELL

jectory with the knife from the front, he'd almost have to be on his knees. But from behind, reaching around her, like this," Danny said, demonstrating in the air, "the upward angle is very natural."

Evan nodded, understanding.

"Also, this." He gently turned her face toward Evan. "These scratches here? To the right of her mouth? Happened at the time of her attack, owing to the very light bleeding and lack of scabbing. There's a good deal of her own skin and a bit of blood under the nails on her right hand. She was right-handed, by the way. So, yeah, she scratched her own face, which tells me the guy had his hand over her mouth. Difficult to do effectively from the front, especially given that he was right-handed as well. We've also got additional DNA from her nails."

Evan nodded. "We need to see if the DNA you pulled from her nails matches what we got from the hair on Bellamy."

"Oh, done deal, right? Much faster than searching for a match in the database. I sent it to Officer Trigg— Deputy?"

"Lieutenant."

"Excellent, so I sent it to her over an hour ago, and she's running it. They've got much cooler equipment over there, I hear."

"Maybe she'll invite you for a field trip some time," Evan said distractedly.

"That would be seriously exciting," Danny said.

"Okay, so anything else notable?"

"Not really. Tox screen is negative everything, save for some Claritin. She had a chicken sandwich for dinner, about three hours before she died. Fried. Fried chicken sandwich." He stared up at the ceiling. "What else?" He looked back at Evan. "Nothing that's really pressing."

Evan reached out and gently turned her face to the front again.

"Her aunt was here earlier," Danny said. "That was bad."

"I'm sure it was," Evan said.

"If I hadn't gotten fed up with *Bones*, you know the forensics show? If I hadn't gotten so aggravated with it, I might have gone into forensic anthropology. That might have been more soothing than what I'm doing right now."

"Maybe you need a little break, Danny," Evan said. "You have any vacation time coming?"

"Oh, right, no. I used it last month to go to a conference on gunshot wounds."

"That sounds less than refreshing," Evan said. "Try the Caribbean next time."

Danny nodded and pulled the plastic sheet back over Tina's face before putting a fist on his hip and looking up at Evan. "That's where the conference was. True enough. Trickery, really."

FOURTEEN

THE NEXT TWO DAYS, Thursday and Friday, were taken up with checking and cross-checking the electronics, mail, financial records and other data collected from the lives of Jake Bellamy and Tina Vicaro, studying the crime scene photos and autopsy reports, and catching up with contacts of both victims who hadn't been available or findable sooner.

None of that turned up anything promising, but Evan and Goff had gone deeper into a background check of Tina's boyfriend, Michael Pittfield, and found that, four years ago, he'd worked for the fishing charter owned by Cindy Babcock's father; the same Cindy Babcock who'd been thrilled to get Evan and Meyers out of her living room.

It was the only connection that they'd been able to find between Bellamy and Vicaro, and it was a weak one in a place the size of Port St. Joe, but it was two-hundred percent more than they'd had the day before.

Evan had assigned deputies to surveil Pittfield round the clock. With any luck, they'd catch him trying to pawn his still-bloody knife, but Evan wasn't planning a party yet.

The DNA under Tina Vicaro's nails had in fact matched that recovered from the hair on Bellamy's body. By Friday evening, Evan was still waiting for a judge to sign a warrant allowing the SO to collect DNA from Michael Pittfield. He wasn't holding his breath.

He got home to his boat just before dark, case files in one hand and two pounds of fresh Gulf shrimp in the other. As he walked down the steps between the Dockside's patio and the fire pit, both already full of people starting their weekends, he saw the back end of Plutes trotting down the dock toward Evan's slip. Evan used to think Plutes wandered around looking for Hannah, but now he wondered if he was just looking for any company better than what he had.

By the time Evan slid his shoes off and went aboard, Plutes was already back inside, stationed at his window. Evan put his shoes in their cubby, noticing as he did that Plutes had once again peed directly in front of his litter box.

Evan opened the glass door into the salon and looked over at the cat, who was looking at him, one ear spasmodically bending toward the back of his head, like something more interesting was right behind him.

"Hello, fatass," Evan said. "I see that you've become bored with peeing inside your litter box again. Perhaps you'd like me to just follow you around with my hand out, so you could pee in my palm, at no inconvenience to yourself."

Plutes narrowed his eyes at him as Evan crossed the salon to the galley, then he went back to looking out the window. Evan stepped down into the galley and put the shrimp in the small sink.

Evan had changed the brand of cat litter he used three times, per the advice of a bunch of nitwits on some cat lady forum. Plutes still chose to pee or poop next to the litter box at least twice a month.

Evan had thought maybe the fuzzy shrimp thing, which he'd suction-cupped to the salon wall, would make Plutes a better person, but the cat actually gave it a wide berth, veering around it by at least five feet, like he thought Evan had loaded it with poison darts.

After changing into sweatpants and a tee shirt, Evan went back up to the salon and turned on some music. His taste ran from classical to 90s alternative and from indie folk to the blues. He wasn't in the mood to get harassed by his own music, so he went for classical. Yo-Yo Ma and Bach's Cello Suite No. 1 in G major. Evan was almost relaxed by the time he stepped back down into the galley.

He grabbed the paper towels, a grocery bag, and his favorite fancy natural cleaner, and stalked back out to the aft deck. He cleaned up the mess, changed the cat litter out while he was at it, and then threw it all away in the can down by the fish cleaning station. When he came back inside, Plutes was sitting on top of the fridge. Evan went back down into the galley, tossed him a glare, then went to the sink.

He rinsed the shrimp, then started breaking off the heads, careful not to lose any of the coral-colored gold that seeped out. The heads he placed in a pot with a little olive oil and butter. The bodies he dried with a dish towel, then put half in a plastic container in the fridge and set the other half aside. Every time he looked up, the cat was still perched on top of the fridge like a raven who'd forgotten his lines. Since Plutes didn't say anything, Evan filled the awkward silence.

"I know you probably think these shrimp heads are for you, but they are not," he said, as he started chopping some onion. "It would benefit you to know that the key to a decent shrimp bisque, or any seafood bisque for that matter, is shrimp heads. I'm going to make stock with those, and that will give me my seafood bisque for dinner tomorrow. You can't have that, because the last time I gave you milk, you threw it up behind the TV."

Evan set the onion aside and started peeling and chopping some garlic. One of his foster parents, one of the early ones, had said he ought to be a prep cook because he liked chopping and dicing so much. Evan had wondered why the guy, who meant well enough, hadn't thought he should be a chef. But cooking did for him what meditation did for others. He wouldn't have wanted to ruin it by doing it for a living.

He set the aromatics to sweating in a pan of melted butter, and the smell of the garlic swayed up toward him like a cobra bent on hypnosis. Evan glanced over to see Plutes, head low, neck craned, like a downhill jumper getting ready to take off. His black nose twitched, and he stared at the small, three burner stove.

"Pay attention, just in case I call one of these days and tell you I need you to start dinner," Evan told him.

· ● ✳ ● ·

Sometime later, after washing the dishes and failing to find anything on TV that wouldn't make him angry or depressed, Evan remembered the cat straightjacket. He went down to his stateroom and grabbed it from his hanging locker, then went back up to the salon to find the cat. He was sprawled on the teak built-in below his favorite window.

The cat almost flipped his lid when Evan picked him up, so rarely had that occurred, but he went limp in Evan's hands until Evan sat on the carpet and tried to wedge him into the halter, which, astonishingly, did not come with instructions for application.

Plutes rabbit-footed him a few times with his back feet and got him good twice with a bite between his thumb and forefinger, but Evan persisted, firmly, but not roughly.

"Would you stop?" he snapped at the cat. "I'm trying to do something nice for you, you jerk."

Evan finally wrangled the cat into the harness, in what he hoped was the proper position. There was a leg sticking out every leg hole and a pissed off face sticking out of the head hole, so Evan figured it was right.

"There!" he said, putting Plutes down on the carpet. "You see?"

Plutes took one step, then sort of melted sideways until he was lying down. Evan stared at him.

"What?" Evan asked. "You can walk. That's what the holes are for."

Plutes didn't look at him. He didn't meow. He didn't growl. He just laid there like he'd been drugged.

Evan leaned over and picked him back up, set him on his feet. "I didn't take your legs."

He let go, and Plutes oozed back over on his side.

Evan sat back on the floor and watched the cat, thinking he was trying to make him feel bad. After a few minutes, neither of them had moved. He wasn't sure the cat had even blinked.

"Are you having a stroke?" Evan asked.

It wasn't quite dawn when Evan rolled onto his back and flung the duvet off his chest. He had finally turned the heat off yesterday, but he'd kept his windows closed, and now the air felt heavy, the room too close.

He blinked a few times, then opened his eyes when he noticed the light in his peripheral vision. Blue light. He got out of bed and leaned over the built-in teak dresser to look out his starboard side window. Across the marina, at least two cruisers were parked on Jetty Park Drive, which went around the back of the marina. They had their lights on, but he hadn't heard any sirens.

There were several short piers jutting out into the bay from the road, along with a few covered pavilions. Between the boats blocking his view and the darkness, Evan couldn't tell what was going on, but it was curious enough to get him up.

He went to the galley and got his espresso going, popped a cup of milk in the microwave, and then went back to his stateroom to get dressed. He pulled on a pair of tan cargo pants and a long-sleeved tee shirt since he planned to shower before work, then went back to the galley, where the aroma of freshly-brewed Bustelo made his amygdala water. As he poured his *café con leche* into his travel mug, he glanced up to see Plutes perched on the ledge that surrounded the galley.

"You'll get your eggs in a few minutes," Evan said as he walked back up to the salon. "Something's afoot over on the jetty."

He grabbed his holster, phone, and badge out of reflex more than anything else and stopped on the aft deck to slip on his deck shoes before stepping to the dock.

He could have swum to his destination faster than he was going to be able to walk it. The spot where the lights were still twirling was only about a hundred yards across the water from his slip. Unfortunately, Evan wasn't one of those lizards that run on water. He'd have to walk all the way around the marina on the plank walkway, then up the short embankment to Jetty Park Road. It would have taken just as long to walk to the parking lot to get his car, so Evan enjoyed his coffee as he made his way over there, at something faster than a stroll, but not in much of a hurry. Most likely, someone had dumped a stolen car, or broken into the car of one of the early-bird fishermen or dumped a washing machine into the bay.

A few other marina residents were making their way to the jetty or just standing topside, peering across the water to see what was going on.

The cruisers were parked sideways in the road, just in front of a covered pavilion that had picnic tables and a restroom for the many locals who liked to fish there. Behind the pavilion was a short pier that jutted out into the water.

Evan's cell rang from his pocket as he was climbing the short embankment.

"Caldwell," he answered without looking, slinging a leg over the short wooden fence.

"Hey, boss, this is Meyers."

"Hey, Meyers, what's up?"

He heard the deputy blow out a frustrated breath. "We got another one."

As Evan crossed the small road, he saw Meyers standing just inside the pavilion with his back to him, phone up to his ear.

"Another what?" Evan asked, though he guessed he already knew.

"Stabbing," Meyers answered. "And this one's in your back yard. Where are you?"

"Behind you," Evan said, and ended the call.

FIFTEEN

MEYERS TURNED AROUND. "Hey, boss."

"Hey."

"So, that guy over there with the silver hair and the tracksuit, he's one of those Loopers, staying here for a week before he heads south again. He was taking his morning walk and found our victim."

Evan looked over to a small group of people off to the right, near the cruisers. One car was Meyers' cruiser, the other was PD. The St. Joe officer was talking to a short, slim man of about seventy, who was visibly shaken.

"Where's the body?" Evan asked.

"Down here."

Evan followed Meyers over to the L-shaped pier.

"Mind the blood," Meyers said, pointing at a softball-sized spot right where the concrete of the pavilion met the wood of the pier. There was another, larger spot on the shallow sand and oyster shell embankment.

There were several large, white rocks right next to the foot of the pier, and Evan spotted some spatter there.

They only went a few steps onto the pier when Meyers stopped and looked over the rail. Evan leaned over to look. There on the ground, about six feet below them was a man's body.

"Well, crap," Evan said quietly.

The man was at least middle-aged, though there wasn't enough light yet to be sure. He had sparse, light brown hair that had previously been covered by the Gators ball cap lying a couple of feet away.

The guy was wearing long cargo shorts and a dark green sweatshirt. His athletic shoes weren't expensive or new, but they were very clean. The man was lying on his left side, but Evan could see that the right side of his sweatshirt was covered in blood. Blood stained the broken oyster shells beneath him and had seeped into the sand.

An expensive-looking fishing pole lay halfway down the embankment. A few feet away sat a red tackle box, on its side but still closed.

"I'm assuming you've already been down there," Evan said.

"Yeah. He's dead," Meyers answered.

"Who else is responding already?"

"EMTs dispatched same time I did, but I was just down the street," Meyers answered. "I was trying to get into work a little early. I heard Forsyth and Summers responding, too."

"Okay. Do me a favor, go grab some tape and start taping this off. Everything from the pavilion to ten yards either side of the pier. Include the guy's car, too."

"Okay."

"Then call Trigg and the ME's office," Evan added. He looked down at the fishing gear. "Looks like he had just gotten here."

"We think so," Meyers said. "The black Saturn on the other side of the pavilion, the trunk is open, got a little cooler in it. Looks like maybe he was gonna go back for that."

"You check the registration?"

"No, I looked, the car's locked. I didn't want to check his pockets for the keys; figured once I saw there was no sign of life I oughta back off."

"Yeah, good work," Evan said distractedly.

"Okay, I'll go get the tape and call Trigg and the ME."

"Thanks," Evan said. "When Summers and Forsyth get here, tell them to block access to the road, from all the way back where it curves. I don't want the looky-loos any closer than that. Hopefully, it's too early for any of the press to be minding the radio."

Meyers started to walk back the way they'd come.

"Hey," Evan called over his shoulder. "Bring me a pair of gloves, would you?"

Evan stood where he was and turned a full circle, slowly. The old man in the tracksuit had been joined by a woman who was undoubtedly his wife. She had both arms wrapped around one of his. Three other men stood just beyond, looking on. Two he recognized from the marina. One he didn't, but that guy was in his bathrobe and accompanied by a terrier on a leash. Nobody suspicious.

He saw another SO cruiser pulling up, as he kept turning. He didn't see anything else on the ground that didn't belong. People were pretty good about keeping the area clean. He saw one Big Red wrapper, but it was sun-faded, clearly not from any time recent. He couldn't see any prints in the ground between the concrete and the embankment. It was mostly shell.

He had come full circle back to the body. He took a couple of gulps of coffee; suddenly the caffeine was more important than it had been twenty minutes earlier. He set the mug down on the wooden railing and was rounding the rail to go down the embankment when he heard Goff behind him.

"Hey, boss," he said. Evan looked over his shoulder. "Meyers asked me to bring you these gloves."

"Thanks, "Evan said, taking them.

"I was on my way in when I heard the call about a body," Goff said. "Meyers says it's another stabbing."

"Yeah," Evan said, pulling on the gloves.

"Casual's kinda a new look for you. Can you think without a suit?"

"You're charming. I walked over here because I saw the lights." He started down to the body. "You coming, or do you need to notify somebody that I'm underdressed?"

"Yeah," Goff answered, which could have meant anything, but he was right behind Evan anyway.

They watched where they stepped, and stopped a few feet past the body, as far as they could get without getting wet. Evan crouched down to look at the man's face and chest.

"Crap."

Goff squatted down next to him, pulling on his own gloves. "Looks like we got another dot to connect."

"Looks like it, based on the wounds," Evan replied. "I can see three wounds for sure, but it's hard to tell, between the blood and the way he's lying. All upper right chest, looks like." He looked over at Goff. "I don't suppose you could be so useful as to know the guy."

Goff shook his head. "Nope."

"I want to wait till Trigg gets here before I mess around getting his ID," Evan said. "Could you call the plates in, find out who this guy is? Black Saturn over there."

"On it," Goff said.

He stood, walked up the embankment on the other side of the pavilion. After a moment, Evan could hear him reciting the plate over his handheld. Meyers came back into his field of vision, yellow crime scene tape in hand.

"Summers has the road blocked," he called down. "Trigg and the ME are on the way."

"Thank you," Evan said, then looked back down at the body. The guy was wearing a nice, but not flamboyant steel watch, worth a good few hundred. No wedding ring and no white line suggesting a missing ring. There was only one defensive wound that Evan could see, on the back of the man's left hand. It looked pretty deep.

Evan reached out and touched the man's neck. He was still warm.

He stood up as he heard a siren. He watched as another PD cruiser appeared. Behind it was Trigg's Jeep, which pulled over and parked just in front of the pavilion. Evan watched and waited as she got out, grabbed her kit from the back, and made her way across the pavilion, eyes fixed on the ground two feet in front of her. She didn't look up until she reached the embankment.

"What'd you do, now?" she asked drily.

"I'm fine, how are you?" Evan asked.

"Disgruntled. Whatever happened to killing people in broad daylight?"

"We're not in Miami, anymore."

Trigg looked around, noting the locations of the blood. "You're telling me," she said, distracted. "If I want a decent Cuban sandwich I have to leave town."

She carefully walked down the embankment, crouched on the other side of the body, and set her kit down on the ground. "Meyers says it looks like the same guy."

"Looks like it," Evan said. He watched her pull on her gloves.

"I suppose it's better than having three stab-happy people running around town."

"That's a nice, positive spin," Evan told her.

"Hey, boss," Goff called as he headed back down. "Car's registered to Mitchell Overstreet. Address over on Hunter Circle."

Evan stood as Goff reached them. "Okay, look. Trigg's just getting started and ME's not here yet. I'm gonna go back to the boat and change. Once Trigg's got her shots of the body, get his ID if he has any, see if it matches."

"Will do," Goff said.

"I'll be back in twenty, tops," Evan said, as he walked back up to the pier and grabbed his mug.

Trigg looked up at him. "Hey, are you making café con leche?"

Evan nodded. "Most likely."

"I don't suppose you could bring me one?"

"Yeah, I can do that."

"Thanks," she said, already back to her camera.

Evan let Meyers know what he was doing and walked past the little group with the PD officer, and the small cluster of law enforcement vehicles. He was just about to climb back over the fence when he spotted Sarah standing with the small group that included the bathrobe guy. She was hugging herself, wrapped up in a pair of sweatpants and a bulky sweater. She was watching him when he saw her.

"Hey," he said quietly, crooking his finger at her. She walked over to him.

"What are you doing here?' he asked.

"Came to see what was going on," she said.

"You don't need to see," he said. He gestured at the fence. "Come on."

"It's another stabbing?" she asked as they climbed over.

"Who told you that?"

"Like eighteen people," she answered.

"Well, this is no place for you," he said. "You don't belong with the dead."

"Seriously? I'm Angel Hardwick's kid," she said. "You think I've never seen a dead body before?"

"Beside the point," Evan said as they started along the walkway. "Go study."

"I have to be at work at seven," she said.

"Then go there," he said, not unkindly.

"You're kinda cranked out," she said. "Not that I blame you."

They walked in silence until they were in front of the wide steps leading up to the Dockside and the marina office, then he touched her arm.

"Hey. You have decent locks on that boat of yours?"

"No, it's a boat," she said. "The locks are crap. Why? Do I need to watch out?"

"I don't think so," Evan answered. "But just keep everything buttoned up at night, okay?"

She looked at him for a moment. "Okay."

Evan nodded, then walked on. He didn't think she was in any danger, at least, not any more than anyone else in town. But three people were dead in less than two weeks.

There was a connection between them, to be sure, but as of this morning, it was looking a lot less likely that the killer was someone the victims had known.

SIXTEEN

TWO HOURS LATER, Mitchell Overstreet's body
had gone off in the back of Danny's van, Trigg had left
for the crime lab, and Evan had endured three minutes
of speaking to a gaggle of reporters who had collected
behind the PD cruiser barricade like Nascar fans watching a tight race.

Evan had shared as much as he could that meant as
little as possible, then had Goff take him to his Honda,
parked behind the Dockside. Then he followed Goff
through a nice, densely-treed neighborhood that Overstreet would not be seeing again.

Mitchell Overstreet's house was neat as a pin, with
manicured, deep green grass, a driveway free of oil stains,
carefully trimmed hibiscus hedges and two white rockers
on the small front porch.

Evan pulled in behind Goff and had just closed his
door when a portly guy with a rim of black hair left on

his pate and a pair of clippers in his hand approached him from the yard next door.

"Can I help you?" he asked, frowning.

"Do you live here, sir?" Evan asked.

"No, I live over there," the man said, gesturing at the yard behind him. "Is everything okay?"

"Do you know Mitchell Overstreet?" Evan asked, again answering a question with a question.

"Well, sure. I mean, to talk to."

"How long have you been neighbors?"

The man thought about that. "Well, he was already here when we moved in four years...no five years ago."

"Does he have a wife? Family? Anyone that lives here with him?"

"No, he lives alone. Can I ask what's wrong?"

"I'm afraid I can't say just now, sir," Evan answered. "But we have his keys and we'll be inside for a little bit, okay?"

"I guess." The man opened and closed his clippers a few times. They creaked a bit, needing some WD-40. "Uh, is he in some kind of trouble? He just left a little while ago."

"When was that?"

"Around five, somewhere around there."

"Did you talk to him?"

"No, I didn't actually see him," the man answered. "I just heard him pull out. My bedroom window's right there," he added, gesturing at the side of his house that faced Overstreet's.

"Was that unusual, for him to leave so early?" Evan asked him.

"No. No, not at all. Not when the weather's decent," the man answered. "He goes fishing pretty much every Saturday morning. Leaves when it's still dark and comes back early afternoon."

Just like Bellamy, Evan thought. "When was the last time you talked to him?"

"Oh, well. We only ever say hello or have a good day or whatever," the man said. "He's nice enough, smiles, you know, but he pretty much keeps to himself. He hardly ever has company."

"Okay, thank you," Evan said. "We're probably going to have another officer stop by and talk to you later today. Will you be home?"

"Yeah, sure," the man said. "I can be. Name's Pete Stein."

"Thank you, Mr. Stein," Evan said.

He walked to the front door, knowing Stein was going to stand there watching, or clipping whatever he was clipping until they had left. Goff came up behind Evan, carrying a satchel of evidence bags and Sharpies. Evan took Overstreet's keys out of the bag in his pocket. It took three tries before he found the one that went to the deadbolt, then the door swung open silently.

Overstreet's house was as neat inside as it was outside. It wasn't so perfect as to be uncomfortably sterile; a pair of loafers waited just inside the door, polished to a sheen, a small recycling box next to the hall closet held a neat stack of newspapers.

The short entryway led into a living room furnished in comfortable-looking pieces. The cherry coffee table shone in the slanted light from between the vertical blinds. There were two books on an end table next to a recliner, and the TV remote was centered on top of those.

Goff turned right to go into a hallway, and Evan walked through the archway at the back of the living room, into a spacious kitchen. It hadn't been remodeled since the nineties, probably, but the appliances and cabinet faces were spotless. There was a dishwasher, but one blue coffee cup, one spoon, and a blue bowl were in the dish drainer on the counter. There were no dishes in the sink.

Against one wall of the kitchen was a built-in desk made of the same material as the counters. Evan went to it. It held a small wooden mail organizer with bills from the electric company, Chase Visa, and Progressive auto insurance in one slot, and a pen and sheet of stamps in the other. Evan didn't remember the last time he'd bought stamps. Auto-payment was one of his few concessions to the modern age.

In the center of the desk was an iPad on a charger. Beneath it, a brown vinyl appointment calendar. When Evan opened it, he found it was one of the ones with two pages per month. It was well-used. Everything was neatly printed in blue ink, and as Evan flipped through the pages, he saw that there were appointments for doctors and barbers and eye exams and pest control services even months ahead.

It seemed that Overstreet used the agenda as a to-do list, as well as an appointment calendar. There were neat entries for things like going grocery shopping, going to the car wash, and picking up dry cleaning.

Evan opened the one drawer in the desk. Push pins, ink pens, rubber bands, pencils, envelopes, and notepads were all in the separate cubbies provided by a silverware organizer. No loose pennies, no twist-ties, no crumpled receipts, and no batteries that might or might not be any good.

Evan closed the drawer gently and looked around the kitchen again. This guy was as neat and organized as anyone Evan had ever met.

He wanted to take pictures of his cupboards to show anyone who ever again accused him of being OCD. So, Evan had five of the same suit, in only two different colors, only kept four place settings and four glasses in the galley, and could tell anyone where the flashlight, the remote and the mail was at any given time? It helped him think clearly, and clearly, he wasn't the only one who needed everything to have a place.

Goff walked in through the living room, carrying a couple of prescription pill bottles.

"Feller's taking Casodex," he said quietly.

"What's that?"

"My brother took it for prostate cancer," Goff said.

That took Evan aback. He didn't even know Goff had a brother. "Is he okay?"

"He passed in oh-two," Goff answered.

"I'm sorry."

Goff nodded. "Yep. There's a desktop computer in the spare bedroom, but no laptop."

"I've got an iPad here," Evan said. He held up the agenda. "And a good old-fashioned datebook. Man after my own heart."

"House is nice, but kinda…tidy," Goff said, looking around the kitchen.

"So's mine," Evan said.

"I don't doubt that," Goff said. Evan looked over to see a bit of a smile on the man's face.

"We need to find out if this guy has family we need to get in touch with," Evan said. "Before the press starts tossing his name around."

"There's some pictures on the wall in the hallway. Two of 'em's got to be his parents, but there's a couple of him and another guy fishing, same guy, and one of a young couple, maybe twenties or so, that looks pretty recent. Wedding picture."

"Okay, let's take pictures of those," Evan said. "Might help us once we get into his contacts, Facebook, whatever."

"Yep," Goff said, and was gone again.

Evan picked up the iPad and agenda, grabbed the Visa bill as well, and started out of the kitchen. Halfway through the doorway, he stopped and put the things on the counter by the sink. Then he walked over to the cupboard next to the sink and opened it.

There were four place settings, blue stoneware, neatly arranged on the bottom shelf. One bowl and one cup were missing. Evan was tempted to put them away for Mitchell Overstreet.

SEVENTEEN

WHEN EVAN GOT TO the office, he was glad it wasn't one of Vi's scheduled Saturdays. He didn't need the lecture. There was a UPS package on the chair next to her desk, never occupied by anyone, ever. Evan leaned over to look at it, saw that it was from Staples, and moved on into his office, closing the door behind him.

He put the things he'd brought from Overstreet's home on his desk, then sat down in his chair. He slid his stack of case files over to the side and then laid out Overstreet's possessions, side by side. The agenda, the iPad, the Visa bill, and the two prescriptions. He'd only brought the two; Goff had found three more, but they were all from the same physician, two for pain and one for sleep. They'd left them in Overstreet's medicine cabinet.

Evan picked up the bag with the prescriptions, then grabbed his office phone and dialed the number. He was surprised to find the office open, but after he told the receptionist who he was, she said she'd have to take a message for the doctor. He left one, stressing that it was urgent.

The iPad was password-protected, as he'd feared. He knew Trigg was in the lab on the other side of the building, and he called her. She picked it up and said she'd run some password programs on it and let him know when she had any luck. Fortunately, she said, iPad passcodes were numeric, and there were only four numbers.

Once she'd gone, Evan had taken off his blazer, hung it on the back of his chair, and gotten to work on the appointment calendar. He noticed once he opened it that it was a two-year calendar, so he had thirteen months to learn about Mitchell Overstreet. What he'd learned, after two hours of going through the calendar and writing down the names of the doctors, phlebotomists, dry cleaners, and miscellaneous service people was that these were the only people in there. No lunch dates with buddies, no dinner dates, or even coffee with a lady. No vacation days noted.

He also learned that the medical appointments had started getting frequent and varied back in June of the previous year. Prior to that, he'd had a doctor's appointment, the same doctor he'd tried to reach, every three months.

Around noon, his office phone rang.

"Caldwell."

"Hey, boss," Goff said. "Nothing in Overstreet's cell phone that matches up with any of the numbers from Vicaro and Bellamy. But we've had better luck on the desktop. No password. Reckon that's cause he lived alone. Anyhow, it's all work stuff. Feller was an accountant."

Evan thought that made perfect sense.

"His tax return's already done, and it's right here," Goff went on. "He works for an accounting firm on Monument. Lucky for us, it's tax season. They're open till three. You want to run over there?"

Evan got up and stuck a hand in his blazer pocket. He dug out his cigarettes and lighter. "Actually, I'm waiting on Trigg and for this guy's doctor to call me back. You want to take it?"

"Sure thing," Goff said.

"Find out if they have any information about relatives, whether he was close with anybody in the office, and whether he's had any problems with anybody, maybe some irate customer who thinks he owes the government too much money."

"Gotcha."

"Sorry, I know you know what we need," Evan said. "Go do it."

"On it," Goff said, and Evan heard his chair squeak in protest as he got up. "Mind if I take Crenshaw?"

"No, go ahead."

Evan felt like he might catch a second wind once he'd walked down the hall to the restroom to pee and rinse his face with a few splashes of cold water.

On his way back down the hall to hit the back door for a smoke, he was hailed by Meyers, who had come in to file his report on finding Mitchell Overstreet.

"Hey, boss!"

Evan stopped in the doorway to the office shared by several deputies. "Yeah."

"Vi was here," Meyers said.

"She still here?"

"Nope, came and went in like two minutes. Must have forgot something when she left yesterday. She asked where you were, though."

Evan winced. "What did you tell her?"

"I said you were in the little law enforcement officers' room," Meyers answered with a smile.

"Thank you," Evan said drily.

Evan continued on down the hall, pushed down on the handle of the back door, and walked out into the bright sunshine. He couldn't help wondering, as he lifted his face to the sun, if Mitchell Overstreet would be heading home about now if someone hadn't stabbed him to death.

He sat down at the little patio table someone had donated for smoking and picnicking and lit his cigarette. His mind vacillated between trying to clear itself and making lists of everything he needed to be sure to do once he got back to his desk. He made it two cigarettes, then went back inside.

Vi's desk appeared to be exactly as it had been earlier. The Staples package remained on the chair. Evan mentally shrugged and walked back into his office. He was halfway to his desk before he saw something foreign on it.

He walked around the desk and sat down in his chair. The appointment calendar had been moved to the left side, below and lined up with the case files. In its place was a square turquoise Tupperware container with a clear lid. On top were a plastic knife and fork wrapped in a paper napkin.

Evan stared at it a moment, then set the cutlery aside and pulled up the lid. It came away with a *thwupping* sound and released a bit of warm air filled with the aroma of curry.

Inside was a healthy scoop of white rice on the left, and a deep yellow stew of shrimp, onion, and what might be sweet potatoes on the right. Evan stared at it a moment.

Of the two of them, Evan had been the cook in his marriage, when he was home to cook or eat. Hannah had a few pasta dishes in her repertoire, but she didn't really enjoy cooking. She frequently met Evan for lunch at a restaurant, but he was pretty sure she'd never made him lunch. That hadn't meant anything to him, but as he sat there looking at this meal that had been left for him, he was touched.

He unrolled the plastic cutlery and took a bite of the curry. It was spicy without being hot, richly flavored, and the only home cooking he'd had in months that he hadn't prepared himself.

He put the fork down in the container and picked up the desk phone. He had to think a minute, then remembered where she'd put the number. It was on the back of a Mary Kay card in his desk drawer. He opened the drawer and fished it out, then dialed the number. It was answered on the third ring.

"This is Vi," she droned.

"You do that at home, too?" Evan asked.

"I'm always Vi," she answered. He could hear a football game in the background. She'd told him once that she recorded all the SEC games she missed working Saturdays and saved them for when football season was over. He hadn't actually believed her. Her cat must have had a phone problem, because he was nearby again, howling.

"Thank you for the curry, Vi," Evan said. "It's delicious."

"Well, don't let it sit. That's vintage Tupperware and it *cannot* be microwaved," she remonstrated him.

"Okay."

"Have a good day, Mr. Caldwell," she said.

"Thank you. You, too."

Just before she hung up the phone he heard her hiss, "Oh, shut the hell up, Mr. Fawlty!"

· ● ✷ ● ·

Goff came back into Evan's office a little over an hour later. He looked tired, and it was one of the few times that Evan remembered the guy was pushing sixty.

"Okay, so I talked to the manager over there at the accounting firm," Goff said as he slid into the chair in front of the desk. "Overstreet's worked there seven years, ever since he moved down from Cincinnati. One of their most popular accountants, she says. Only missed four days of work since he's been there, which is really saying something."

"Okay."

"He has a brother named Rob back in Ohio, who was his emergency contact."

"We need to call him," Evan said with a sigh.

"I did."

"Geez. Thank you," Evan said.

"I figured you were full up on next of kins for the month," Goff said. "Brother's all beat to hell about Mitchell. He moved down here after he survived prostate cancer, wanted to enjoy fishing and whatnot in the Sunshine State. Last year they found more. He was fighting, but it wasn't looking good. Now some piece of work took whatever he had left away from him, which really rusts my bucket."

"Man."

"Yeah. Anyhow, the brother's getting a flight out of Ohio in the morning," Goff went on. "He's got to make arrangements for someone to take care of the two kids he has at home. That wedding picture on the wall, that was the older son. The brother's. I texted him the pictures from the wall. The fishing pictures are the two brothers. Rob comes down twice a year to fish with Mitchell."

"Did you ask him if Overstreet had talked to him about any problems with anyone?"

"I did. He didn't. Overstreet called him every Sunday evening but never had a whole lot to say. They talked about work and the brother's kids and the cancer and what fish Overstreet had been catching. He liked his fishing."

"Okay." Evan rubbed a hand over his face.

"He gave me a few people to call and talk to. One's a lady he dated for a few months back four or five years ago. They were more or less companions, the brother tells me, and she moved down to Cape Coral and that was that. Another one is a guy he goes inshore fishing with every now and then. Brother only had his number cause the guy gave Mitchell a ride to the oncologist when he was feeling pretty bad."

"Have you called them?"

"No, that's what I'm fixing to do now," Goff answered. "How are you faring on your end?"

"Trigg got into the guy's iPad, but it's just Netflix, a bunch of fishing apps and a ton of Kindle books. Still waiting for anything she got from the scene." Evan swung his chair slowly to the left, then to the right. "I haven't heard back from the doctor, but now that we have next of kin and we know what was going on medically, he probably won't be much help."

"Anything from that date book?"

"Not really. The guy had no social life at all."

Goff nodded, tugging at each end of his mustache.

"Danny's got a lot on his plate today," Evan said. "Apparently three people were brought in late last night from a single vehicle wreck over in Wewa. He says he probably won't have anything until Monday morning, but from what he said at the scene, he's betting it's the same guy."

"Ain't nobody gonna put good money down on that bet," Goff said.

"No." Evan sighed. "Okay, go ahead and make those calls. I'm going to go grab Vicaro's and Bellamy's laptops again. We're missing the connection here, and there is one."

"You ever work a serial before? 'Cause that's what we might be looking at here if we can't find something ties these folks to one another."

"No, I haven't. But I do know that the victims of serials, by and large, fit a certain profile. The only characteristics all *three* of these people have in common is that they seem to have been nice, normal people. Who were killed while they were doing something that was a regular part of their routine. Bellamy ran every Saturday. Vicaro worked second shift for the last sixteen months. And Overstreet went fishing every Saturday morning that he could. Possibly to the jetty."

"So, you're thinking this guy's watching these folks, picking his best opportunity."

"Oh, yeah," Evan sighed as he stared at his desktop. "He's watching them. We just don't know why."

Evan was pulling into Sunset Bay late in the afternoon when he realized that he had forgotten to visit Hannah the day before. It stunned him so thoroughly that he'd sat in the car, staring out the windshield for several minutes.

In 291 days, not one had gone by without him sitting or standing at her bedside, even if only for thirty minutes. A very small part of him thought that she never knew he was there, that she didn't hear him rectifying his failure during the previous four years to communicate with her about his day, something she had often mentioned to him.

But another part of him sat there in the car, frozen by guilt, believing that she had noticed yesterday and that she had thought it typical of him to be absent. It surprised him to realize that part of what kept him in the car was his uncertainty about what he should say, of how to justify his being so wrapped up in the case that he had not only forgotten to come see her but failed to notice that he'd forgotten.

Eventually, he'd gone inside, and when he'd stood at her bedside, he'd simply apologized. No justification, no explanation, just a simple apology that felt simultaneously inadequate and unnecessary. When he'd driven back out of Sunset Bay, he'd felt the weight of guilt in his chest, been so uncomfortable looking at himself in the rearview mirror, that he'd decided he needed to get out on the water before he found himself indulging in an evening of self-serving malaise.

There was still a good hour of daylight left when he got to the marina, so he quickly went down to his state-room to change. He hung his suit blazer in the hanging locker, where it brushed up against the dry-cleaning bag holding his sheriff's uniform. Technically, he was supposed to wear it, but as a lieutenant in charge of the Criminal Investigations Department, back in Brevard County and now here, he'd been allowed to wear a suit, and he had no desire to change that.

He'd worn the uniform once, at Hutchens' funeral, and felt particularly awkward in it given he was attending the service of the man who'd worn the same uniform just previously. Quillen had mentioned the lack of uniform twice, but then had let it go, telling Evan that at least he looked 'more Fed than flunky.' Evan didn't think any of his guys in uniform looked like flunkies, but he let that go, too.

Once he'd changed into cargo pants and a sweater, Evan grabbed a bottle of water from the fridge and went

out to the aft deck. The harness that had been so spec-
tacularly useless the night before hung on the doorknob
and jingled against the glass as he opened the door. Plutes
was curled on top of the grill, soaking up the heat of the
sun-warmed metal cover.

Evan hopped from his dive platform to the Sea Fox's
bow and walked back to the cockpit. He hopped down
and had just finished checking the oil reservoirs for the
twin 115 Suzuki 4 strokes when he heard a soft thump
on the bow. He stood up and craned his neck to see
Plutes sitting near the bow pulpit like a hood ornament.

"Come on," Evan complained as he walked up to the
bow. "I don't have much daylight left."

Plutes flattened his ears as Evan heaved him up and
dropped him over the side onto the dock. A few minutes
later, after he'd dropped the propellers, checked his
fuel, and started the engines priming, he looked up to
find Plutes situated back on the bow, this time looking
through the windshield at Evan like he was waiting for
Evan to tell him to get the bowline.

Evan sighed and stared at the cat a moment, then
moved forward to evict him again, but Plutes jumped
to the dock on his own. Evan pursued him, snatched
him up, and put him in the salon, making sure to close
the window he always left open for the cat to get to the
litter box. It would probably mean he'd come home to
some sort of urinary statement, but at least he wouldn't
have to fetch the cat out of the Gulf.

It occurred to him, as he was motoring out toward the St. Joseph Peninsula, that if he was going to be saddled with a cat, one who seemed to enjoy boating was as good as he could expect.

Once Evan had rounded the north end of the peninsula and entered the Gulf proper, he felt himself beginning to relax. He opened the throttle up and smiled as the bow bounced gently through the waves. Growing up in Miami, Evan had started surfing when he was eight, thanks to a foster brother who was an avid surfer. In surfing, Evan had found a release that he hadn't been able to duplicate in any other way.

He still had two boards, crammed against the bulkhead in the V-berth, but he'd only surfed twice since he left his favorite breaks in Cocoa Beach. Both times, he'd made the short trek out to St. George Island.

While it was no substitute for the intimacy between man and wave that surfing provided, getting out on the Sea Fox and opening her up was a decent stand-in. As the wind battered his ears and a light sea spray coated his skin, he felt himself relaxing, leaving the dead bodies and missed connections and silent, disappointed wives behind him, if just for a little while.

EIGHTEEN

FIRST THING MONDAY morning, Evan stood at the front of the small, and rapidly shrinking, conference room. About a dozen-and-a-half steely faces stared back at him. If the room had been larger, there would have been more. The PSJ chief of police stood silently in the back of the room, flanked by two investigators from the Florida Department of Law Enforcement. Chief Beckett from Wewahitchka and one of his officers were propping up another corner of the wall. The other sets of eyes belonged to Evan's deputies, and the PSJ police officers assigned to the expanding Bellamy et al Taskforce.

Evan understood what the presence of the state investigators meant – his time to solve this was running out. One more body and they would take over. Evan couldn't justify his resentment – somebody had to stop the murders and so far, he had failed – but he felt it nonetheless. As he prepared to address the crowd, his mind reviewed the moves he had made since finding Bellamy. There was nothing the state investigators could have done that he hadn't tried. He gratefully accepted their offer to help, but did not, in the least, feel that the responsibility to solve the case had been lifted from him.

Beckett's presence was also unsettling. The Wewa Chief had called and offered any assistance Caldwell might want. Evan needed the manpower but couldn't quite decide how he felt about Beckett. He had asked Beckett to send over an officer if he could spare one – Wewahitchka only boasted a police department of four– but he had tried to hint that the chief's presence was not required. As they eyed each other from either end of the room, Evan realized that was probably exactly why Beckett had decided to attend.

Goff had started the meeting with a quick synopsis of the case so far, bringing the newcomers up to speed, filling in all the details Evan had not provided to the media, and correcting the numerous inaccuracies the media had concocted to replace that missing information. Now, Evan stepped up to introduce material that would be new to everybody.

"I've just returned from meeting with the M.E. or, with his assistant, that is. No surprises there. Mr. Overstreet's wounds indicate that he was killed by the same person who killed Bellamy and Vicaro. The size and shape of the blade match. The angle of attack indicates that whoever attacked Overstreet was the same height as the person who attacked the other two. More than enough similarities to say it is our guy.

"There are a few differences. Overstreet was attacked from the front. Vicaro, from behind. Bellamy *may* have been attacked from the front, or the side, though he was stabbed from several different angles. However, in each case, the killer focused his attack on the upper right torso." Evan used a pointer to tap at diagrams depicting the locations of the wounds on each victim.

"Another, worrisome difference," Evan continued, "Overstreet had fewer stabs than Vicaro. Vicaro had fewer than Bellamy. Overstreet also had fewer defensive wounds, and the killer left almost no forensic evidence at this third attack." Evan pause to let the team assimilate what he had said. "That means he's getting better, more efficient, and probably more comfortable. It means, unless we can find the connection between these victims, we're going to have a whole lot more."

"Connection?" Deputy Holland scoffed. "It's a young, single woman, a middle-aged loner, and a family man from out of town. Totally different profiles, totally different groups of friends. This guy," Holland said, waving a hand at Overstreet's picture, "didn't even *have* friends."

"There has to be a connection. These are *not* random victims. He chose them, stalked them, was lying in wait for each of them," Evan said. "The fact that Overstreet has no social contacts means that whatever ties these three together is probably more likely to be a professional contact of some sort, rather than a personal one. "

"The news is all over this, but they haven't even given this guy a nickname," Holland argued back, "because there *is no* common thread."

"Except that he stabs all his victims in the same place," Goff said. That tickled something in Evan's mind, but he lost the thought before he could lock onto it.

"How about 'the Saint Joe Stabber,'" Beckett suggested, sounding amused, "not too original, but it does have a bit of a ring to it."

"Don't give them any ideas," another deputy put in.

Somebody chuckled. Mutters and whispers rippled through the crowd. Evan heard somebody ask, "Why the right side? You'd think he'd go for the heart." To which another replied, "Maybe he's dyslexic." Someone else was still fixated on the name. "What about, Joe the Ripper?"

Evan knew that an outside observer would think the remarks cold and inappropriate to the loss of life, but he also knew that they weren't making the remarks because they didn't care. They were simply distancing themselves, objectifying the victims in a way, yes, but in order to not be distracted by their humanity.

"We ain't here to name him," Goff snapped. His voice was quiet, but it quieted every other voice in the room. "We're here to identify him and sack him up."

"We've had a murder every three to four days," Evan said. "He watches these people and knows their routines, so he is an opportunistic killer, but if we simply look at the time between murders, he's due to kill again tonight or tomorrow. We can *not* let that happen. You each have an assignment. The connection is in there somewhere." He indicated the files stacked neatly by the door. "Somehow, somewhere, these three people crossed this man's path, and we've got to find that path."

· ● ✳ ● ·

Hours later, after talking with several local contacts who knew Mitchell Overstreet, going over to the bullpen to spend wasted time on the man's desktop, and dragging his eyeballs through the reports from task force members, Evan felt no closer to finding a reason for even one of the killings, much less all three.

In one part of his mind, he'd felt like he'd missed it, and in another, he felt like its discovery was imminent, like watching the horizon for land, certain that he'd charted his position properly and only needed to stare long enough to know he'd found his destination.

Late in the afternoon, his eyes weary from printed and pixelated text, Evan set the deputies' reports and his own case files aside, in their separate stacks, neatly lined up with the top left corner of his desk. Then he grabbed a bottle of water from the break room, stretching his legs as a bonus, and came back to his desk.

He took a few swallows of water, stared at the two neat piles of paperwork, and tried to decide which piece of this case he wanted to go over for the tenth or fifteenth time. He'd stacked his files in reverse chronological order, with Overstreet on top. When he opened it, the brown agenda was on top, and he almost felt like handwritten notes would be a refreshing change, so he slipped it out and opened it to the first two pages, January of the prior year.

Deep down, he was certain that this was going back too far, but he hoped, weakly, that some pattern would emerge that he hadn't noticed when looking for individual bits of information. He'd reached November by the time he'd decided that he'd been too optimistic but, having gone that far, he committed to finishing.

He was looking at his last two pages, for the current month, when he found himself vaguely bothered by two entries. The first, on Thursday the 13th, was a note to renew his license online. The second, on Monday the 17th, was a note to go to the DMV.

The first notation stuck out at him because it had several blue lines drawn through it. Other notations, appointments, and reminders throughout the book that had been crossed out had been done so with one neat, blue line.

As Evan looked at the two notes simultaneously, he concluded that the first task was actually scratched out, undone, rather than completed. That bugged him somehow, but he didn't know why. Something niggled at him, like a mosquito that had landed but not yet bitten, but staring at the pages wasn't producing a reason.

Finally, frustrated, he grabbed his cigarettes and lighter from his lap drawer, told Vi he was going out for a smoke, and hit the back door.

He was sick to death of sitting, so Evan paced around the concrete picnic set. He cupped a hand over his lighter to shield it from the light breeze and lit up. He took his first, long drag as he tucked his smokes into his pants pocket, then stood staring at the backs of the private vehicles belonging to staff members, his own Pilot, and the Culligan water truck.

He was reminded, for probably the fourth time, that he had wanted to ask the guy about getting the water delivered to his boat. He could put the dispenser in front of the sink in the V-berth, which was just forward of the galley, and it would save him using up all his bottled water for his coffee. City water was fine for cooking and the cat, but beneath his consideration for his *café con leche*.

He didn't want the distraction of actually having a conversation with the guy once he came back out, so Evan pulled his wallet from his back pocket, fished out a business card from his auto insurance agent, grabbed his pen from his shirt pocket, and jotted down the number on the side of the Culligan truck. He was jamming the card back into its slot when his eye was caught by his driver's license, crammed into the little plastic window that never comfortably accommodated any license known to man.

He didn't know why he was looking at it, why it had caught his attention, but that niggling was there again, so he read. His name, Evan Patrick Caldwell. The address of the marina. Height: 6'1. Weight: 170, though he suspected he might have gained a pound or two since getting his Gulf County license back in September. And that's when it hit. The thought that had been eluding him all day burst in his brain with sudden clarity.

In his haste to shove his wallet back in his pocket, he dropped it, cursed and was already running for the back door when he snatched it up.

He hurried soundlessly down the carpeted hallway and charged into Vi's office. She looked up sharply, her big dragonfly earrings trembling.

"What's happened?" she demanded to know.

It killed Evan to pause, but he did. "Get hold of Goff. I think he's in the bullpen. Tell him to get over here quick."

He didn't wait for her to answer, just hurried on into his office. He slid the agenda to the side and pulled his case files toward him. He opened Overstreet's to the second page, where the copy of his license was secured. The real license was in his wallet in the evidence room. Evan set it to one side, pulled Vicaro's file on top of that, and found the corresponding page in her file. His intercom buzzed. He mashed at the button with one finger, striking twice before he got it.

"Yeah."

"This is Vi. Sgt. Goff is mid-urination and will be here momentarily."

"Okay."

Evan grabbed Bellamy's file and had just folded back the cover page to expose his copied license when Goff opened the door and scurried in, every single thing on his gun belt rattling like a broken wind chime.

"What's up?" he asked as he hurried to the desk.

"Check this out," Evan said excitedly. "We have a commonality. All three of them!"

Goff came around the desk to stand next to Evan and look at Bellamy's file. "What?"

"Look," Evan pointed with his finger. "The Bellamys just moved here, right? He got his Gulf County license December 6th."

"Okay," Goff said as Evan shoved Bellamy's file aside to expose Vicaro's.

"Tina Vicaro lost her wallet, remember? Look. She replaced it January 14th." He shoved that file aside. "Look at Overstreet. He renewed his license on the 17th."

Evan looked over at Goff, smiling. He felt a relief that was so similar to joy as to be almost indistinguishable.

"Well, damn," Goff said quietly. "If we got a rampaging killer on our hands, only makes sense he hangs out at the DMV."

"Bet you a hundred he works there. Maybe he was the one that handled all three."

"I won't have a hundred till Wednesday," Goff said, "and I ain't that stupid."

"We need to find out who took care of each of the three victims," Evan said.

"Well, you're in luck," Goff said. "My cousin Audrey's the supervisor."

Evan grinned at him. "I knew having you around would pay off eventually."

Goff nodded, pulling a stick of gum out of his shirt pocket. "Well, it was never gonna be about the sex, that's for sure."

Evan looked at his watch. It was sneaking up on five. "What time do they close?"

"Five-thirty."

"Come on." Evan stalked around his desk, Goff on his heels. "Call her up. Tell her we need her to stay late and wait for us. I want to know when the last employee is out of there."

Vi looked up as they hurried past her desk and frowned over her bifocals at them.

They walked briskly down the carpeted hall toward the front of the building. Goff spoke quickly into his phone behind him, accompanied by the percussion of his gun belt.

Evan pushed open the glass door to the Sheriff's Office. Goff stopped just before the door to finish his conversation, as Evan walked over to the top of the front steps. Goff came out a moment later and came to stand next to Evan.

"She's good to go. She says everybody's in a hurry to leave once the clock strikes. Place should be clear by quarter-till at the latest."

The two men stood there, Evan with his hands on his hips, Goff rubbing two fingers over his mustache.

"Maybe we should just mosey across the parking lot, go in there, and ask him to reveal himself," Evan said, as they stared at the front entrance of the courthouse, which also housed the DMV, less than a hundred yards away.

NINETEEN

EVAN LOITERED IN THE reception area of the
SO for the next thirty-five minutes, staring out the big,
plate-glass window that looked out onto the parking lot
in front of the courthouse. They'd sent Crenshaw over to
the round concrete table beneath a palm near the courthouse entrance. It wasn't unusual for an officer to hang
out there on his lunch break, and Crenshaw was able
to take pictures on his phone of every male that left the
building after five o'clock. He also noted car makes and,
when possible, license numbers.

Even though Evan knew they had no way of knowing
the difference between a lawyer, a DMV clerk and a guy
with jury duty, Evan wanted the pictures. He had this
horrible fear that their guy would get the heebie-jeebies
that very day and take off and that once they'd identified
him, all they would have was an employee file containing a fake plate number and a false address.

Finally, at twenty before six, Goff's cousin called and told them everyone had left the office. Evan grabbed Goff, and they walked over to the courthouse, releasing Crenshaw from his post as they headed for the front door. The security guard started to tell them everybody was closed, but Evan told him they were meeting someone and, after the requisite security check, they made their way to the DMV.

When they got to the door, a glass door tinted faintly green, Evan saw a short, slim woman in her fifties, with black curly hair and big round glasses leaning against the front counter, watching them.

"That's Audrey," Goff said unnecessarily as she hurried to let them in.

She unlocked it for them and held it open. "Hey, Ruben," she said as they walked in. "Sheriff."

"Evan," he said in response. "Thank you for waiting for us."

"Sure thing," she answered, closing and locking the door. "I was just gonna go do some target shooting later," she said.

Evan looked over at Goff. "Are you a whole family of gun cranks?"

Goff had been a sniper in the Army, and once told Evan he could shoot the stink off a squirrel fart from two-hundred yards. His wife was known to carry a 50cal Desert Eagle, though Evan couldn't imagine her stick arms holding the thing steady.

"Some people fish, some people watch TV, we shoot," Goff said. "Famous for it. Ain't nobody in my family ever been broken into."

They were following Audrey down a short hallway. At the end of it was an office with the light on and the door open.

"Sheriff, Ruben says you need to know about one of my employees?" Audrey asked.

"Well, it's not quite that direct," Evan said. "We don't know which employee yet."

"How can I help?"

She led them into the office. There was one orange vinyl chair in front of her desk, and another by the door. Evan sat in the former, while Goff dragged the latter over.

"We have three people who have been here at the DMV in the last month and a half," Evan said as she sat down behind her desk. "They all got new or renewed licenses. We need to find out who took care of them. Is that tracked by terminal or by employee?"

"By employee," she answered. "They don't always work at the same computer, so it's tracked by employee number."

"Okay. Can we pull these licenses and see who printed them or issued them or whatever?"

"Sure. I can do that from right here," she said. "Do you have the license numbers?"

Evan pulled a slip of paper out of his shirt pocket, on which he'd had Vi note the last names and license numbers. He handed it to her.

She took it, glanced at it quickly, then started tapping away on her keyboard. After a moment, she sat forward a bit to peer at the screen. "Okay, this first one, Overstreet. Employee number four-one-six. That's Enid Franklin." She looked over at Evan, a little sternly. "She's a good friend of mine."

"That's okay, we're not looking for a female."

Mollified, she turned back to her computer and started typing again. "Vicaro. That was five-oh-nine. Larry Winters." She looked up at Evan, who scribbled the name down in his notebook.

She looked at the last name on the notepaper, then slowly looked back up at Evan. "Wait a minute," she said quietly. "These are those people that were killed."

"Yes, ma'am."

She looked at Goff.

"What about the last one?" Goff asked her.

She looked it up. "Bellamy's license was issued by employee three-five-seven." She looked up at Evan. "Sam Kovacs."

Evan wrote it down, then sat there tapping his pen on the notebook. "We were really thinking the same person served all three," he said.

"No."

"Okay, but they were all here," Evan said. "Even in a town this size, that's too much coincidence. You have video cameras out there, right?"

"Yes, of course."

"Does it show on there what time each license was issued?"

"Yes, the entries are all time-stamped."

"How far back do you keep your video?" Evan asked her, praying for an answer he liked.

"Oh, way back. It's all digital, and it's all backed up, oh, I think eighteen months. I don't handle that, that's all from the state security office."

"Okay," Evan said, daring to feel excited again. "Can you get us the footage from say, an hour before to an hour after each visit?"

Her face fell. "I'm sorry, I don't know how I would do that. Each file is automatically saved by date, but I don't have any software for editing it or anything. All I can do is download each zip file to a jump drive for you."

"That's okay, don't worry. That'll be great, thank you," Evan said. "I need one other thing, to help us narrow down what we're looking for on all this video."

"Sure."

"How many employees do you have, counting everybody? Receptionist, clerks, security guard, whomever."

"Just fourteen," she said. "As DMVs go, we're not real big."

"Can you find out which employees worked all three of those days?"

"Sure, but it's probably going to be most of them."

"That's okay, too," Evan reassured her. "Eliminating anyone at this point will save us time, and we really need to save as much as possible."

DAWN LEE MCKENNA & AXEL BLACKWELL

"Okay."

"You can also skip your female employees unless one of them is at least six feet tall," Evan added.

"No, I know for a fact that Emily's the tallest woman here, and she's only five-seven," Audrey answered.

"Okay."

"We have…" Audrey looked up at the ceiling a moment. "We have six male employees."

"Okay, that helps," Evan said. "Six is better than fourteen."

A few minutes later, accessing her payroll software, Audrey had their answer. "All six of them worked all three of those days."

Evan sighed. "One was the answer I was hoping for."

"There aren't that many government jobs in town," she said. "You got one, you hang onto it by not missing work."

"Okay, can I get a printout or something with those six employees' names?"

She chewed at the corner of her lip. "Can I get in trouble for giving you that without a warrant?"

"No, I don't think so. I could hang out here tomorrow morning and get that information just by looking at the nameplates on their stations."

"That's true," she said. "I'm wondering, though, if I can get in trouble for the video."

Evan thought about that a moment. "You know what? Even if we get this guy, saying he's one of your employees, even if we get him, the video isn't going to be a big point in court. We're not going to be using it to try to convict him, we're just using it to figure out how we need to get the evidence that *will* convict him."

She looked at Evan, then at Goff, then back at Evan. "That sounds like crap to me," she said.

"It might be," Evan told her.

She thought for just a few more seconds. "Well, if the higher-ups get wind of it and they want to write me up, they can. I've got almost twenty years here with a clean record."

"Just tell 'em you'll go on the news talking about how the state cares more about not looking bad than they do about protecting the public," Goff said. "That oughta do it."

She blew out a breath. "I don't think they're gonna know, anyhow," she said. "Just never mind."

A few minutes later, she had downloaded the zip files of the appropriate days' videos onto a jump drive and handed Evan a printout containing the names of the six employees. Evan knew enough to know he couldn't ask for socials or other personal data, but he didn't think some anecdotal information would be out of line.

"What can you tell me about each of these guys? What do they do here, that kind of thing."

"Well, let's see. Mike Westmoreland is a clerk. He's about to retire. Next week, actually."

"How old is he?" Evan asked as he took notes.

"Almost seventy. He couldn't afford to leave any sooner. They need his wife's social security, too, and she just turned sixty-five."

"Okay," Evan said.

"Peter Bullock is very nice, he and his boyfriend or whatever just finished a big fundraiser for the animal shelter, and he's always talking about some little dog they've adopted." She looked at the list upside down. "Scott Waller is a good employee, very quiet. He's the photographer, usually, unless we're backed up, then everybody takes their own pictures and he has to man a terminal. Sam Kovacs is an ass."

"How so?"

"He's just a jerk," she said, shrugging. "Not too many people like him. He's okay with the customers, but he's always bragging about one thing or another with the rest of us."

"What's he do here?"

"He's a clerk. Dane Little is a nice guy, he's a clerk, too. His son's been giving him a lot of heartache, poor guy." She looked at Evan knowingly. "Drugs."

Evan noted it.

"Who else?" She looked at the list again. "Oh, John Crawford. He's the security guard. He's okay. I don't really know him well. He was just hired right before Christmas. We had to replace the last guy, Norman Lewis. He got caught posting pictures of his inappropriate parts on Craigslist," she said with a grin. "In uniform, 'cause he was a moron, I guess."

Evan thought that was interesting. Apparently, Goff did, too, because he was smiling at the wall behind Audrey.

"Okay, Audrey, thank you," Evan said. "I can't think of anything else you can help us with at the moment, so we'll let you go home." She stood up, and they stood with her. "I will ask you not to mention this to anyone, though. No one here, none of your friends…you understand, I'm sure."

"I get it," she said. "Look, I hope you guys find out nobody here did something that awful."

"So do we," Evan said. It was a lie. He hoped down to his shoes that someone there was their guy. It was all they had.

TWENTY

AT JUST AFTER five-thirty the next morning, Evan went for his first run in almost two weeks, a long time for him. He'd debated skipping it that morning, too, given that there was going to be a lot of information to go through when he got to work, but he needed his head clear for that precise reason and decided it was worth the half hour.

There was a small park next to the marina, connected by a path, that Evan usually used for his runs. The Cape San Blas lighthouse was there, and there was an excellent trail. Between getting to the park and jogging its perimeter, he got enough of a run to get his systems flowing, but not so much that he was exhausted when he finished.

When he got back to the boat, he took a quick shower, put on his last clean suit, made a second cup of coffee, and whisked up some eggs. He was in the middle of cooking them when his cell rang. Picking it up off the counter, he saw that it was Goff.

"Hey," he answered, holding the phone with his head.

"What are you doing?" Goff asked.

"Scrambling the cat's eggs," Evan answered without thinking.

There was a moment of silence.

"Well, when you're done with that curious task, get on in here," Goff said. "Trigg left our videos for us."

"Awesome," Evan said. "I'll be there in ten."

He disconnected the call. When they'd gone back to the office the night before, he'd pressed Trigg into service locating the time stamps they were looking for, then copying clips that contained everything from half an hour before each license was issued to half an hour after. She'd griped, since she was planning on leaving early, but Evan knew she wasn't that annoyed. She was as much of a workaholic as he was.

He'd been there himself until almost seven, assigning a couple night shift guys the tasks of running background checks on each of the male employees and printing out their driver's licenses.

Evan turned off the gas burner and removed the small skillet from the heat. When he turned around, Plutes was sitting on the teak ledge over the sink. Evan grabbed his stainless-steel bowl out of the dish drainer and scooped the eggs into it. By the time he put the bowl down on the lobster placemat by the dinette, Plutes was right beside him.

"It's hot," Evan said, straightening. Plutes went to it, anyway, grabbed a bite, and immediately dropped it onto the placemat.

"I don't understand," Evan told him. "You just heard me tell you it was hot."

· ● ✳ ● ·

When Evan got to the SO, he could feel the energy in the air. There wasn't a lot of noise or motion, there weren't six simultaneous conversations going on about the case, but the expectation of results, of being able to end this thing soon, could be felt like static electricity.

In the bullpen, he found Crenshaw and Meyers each viewing separate video files. Crenshaw had the one for Bellamy's visit to the DMV, and Meyers the one for Vicaro's.

"How's it going, guys?" he asked them as he walked in.

"You know what?" Meyers asked. "The only thing worse than going to the DMV is watching everybody else go to the DMV."

"I imagine," Evan said. "Anything yet?"

"Tina Vicaro's still waiting in line here," answered Meyers. "So far, she's talked to the security guard, the new one, not Lewis the Lefty."

Crenshaw pointed at his screen. "Bellamy's at the counter now. He was waited on by Sam Kovacs."

"That's the guy that's supposed to be a jerk, right?"

"Yeah, and he is. I went to high school with him," Crenshaw said. "I wouldn't figure him for our guy, though. Couldn't say why, just my thought."

"He talk to anybody else while he's there?"

"So far, just the lady that was in line in front of him, older African-American lady with a service dog. Looked like they were talking about the dog."

"Okay," Evan said. He looked at the wall beside them. Six photocopies of driver's licenses were pinned to a corkboard that had previously held outdated missing persons flyers and notices from HR. "These our male employees?"

Crenshaw looked up. "Yeah. Peters said the background reports are on your desk."

"Thanks," Evan said. "Seen Goff?"

"He just left like five minutes ago," Meyers piped up. "Been here since five. He went out to Weber's."

Weber's was a family-run donut place out on Cape San Blas, and it would have been the best place in the county even if it wasn't the only one. Evan knew from experience that Goff had a thing about being there when they opened the doors at seven-thirty. He looked at his watch. Seven-twenty. Yeah, Goff was dusting the front window with his mustache about now. He didn't begrudge the man the forty-minute jaunt; everybody had been putting in late, early, and extra hours, particularly Goff.

"Okay, thanks guys," Evan said. "I'm gonna go take a look at these people. Let me know when anything interesting comes up."

Vi was already at her desk when he got there. She was usually scheduled to work seven to five, but he'd been there as early as six and always found her already there.

"Mr. Caldwell," she addressed him, frowning over her bifocals. "The background checks you requested are on your desk."

"Good morning, Vi," he said. "Thank you."

"You also have a message from James Quillen," she added. "It's urgent, as is customary."

"What does he want?"

"He wants you to tell him that people have stopped stabbing other people, immediately."

"He wants me to tell him that immediately, or he wants them to stop immediately?"

She stared at him a moment.

"Do me a favor, call him back and tell him I don't have time to call him back because I'm looking for stabbers."

He headed for his office door. He was about to close it when he heard Vi ask someone for Commissioner Quillen. He smiled as he shut the door.

Evan spent the next hour going through the background checks run on the six males who had worked all three of the days the victims had been there. None of them had felony records, but Evan supposed that was a prerequisite for county employment. All of them also had clean licenses, which didn't come as a surprise, either.

Sam Kovacs, who had moved to the area in the nineties, when he was fourteen, did have a misdemeanor disturbing the peace, but it was from spring break in Daytona, 2001. Every male that had ever been there had one of those. Evan hoped he was their killer based solely on his dislike for the smirk the guy wore in his photo.

He was going over Kovacs' credit report, which was amusing, when his intercom buzzed. He reached out and pressed the button as he turned the page. "Yeah."

"This is Vi," he heard Goff say.

Evan smiled. "Where's Vi?"

"Smoke break."

"What's up?"

Goff opened his door. "We got us a common denominator, as it were."

"The videos?"

"Yep."

Evan followed Goff down the hall and back to the office where Crenshaw and Meyers were sitting there smiling, each one holding a donut. Crenshaw had confectioners' sugar on his uniform shirt, and Evan didn't even mind.

"What'd you get?" Evan asked as he and Goff walked in.

"Look here," Meyers said. Evan went to stand beside Meyers' chair, leaned on his desk. Goff had apparently seen it already, or he had the eyesight of a mantis shrimp, because he stayed in the doorway, smiling.

"This guy here," Meyers said, pointing at a zoomed in and therefore pretty fuzzy picture of a man standing at the end of the counter. "The photographer. What's his name, Pete?"

"Waller," Evan and Crenshaw said simultaneously.

"Yeah. He's the only one interacted with all three of our victims," Meyers said. "Took all three pictures."

Evan straightened up and smiled over at Goff. Goff smiled back.

"You want me to go stand in the window and surveil him?" he asked.

Crenshaw snorted powdered sugar onto his desk.

"Some days, this job is really, really crappy," Evan said to the room at large. "And some days, it's really, really good."

TWENTY-ONE

GOFF FOLLOWED EVAN back to his office. Vi glanced up at them as she tapped at her keyboard but said nothing as they hurried past her. Evan quickly sat at his desk and pulled Waller's file out of the stack.

"Okay, the guy lives on Cypress Avenue," Evan said. He looked up at Goff. "Where's that?"

"Over by the elementary school."

"He's at two-thirty-three Cypress. What time is it?"

"Almost nine-thirty."

"So, he's at work," Evan said. "Get somebody to drive over there, scope out where we can put surveillance. I want somebody on the house 24/7, and somebody on *him*, even if they're just sitting out in our parking lot staring at the courthouse."

Goff walked out of the office, and Evan flipped through Waller's background report for several minutes. It failed to give him anything more interesting than he'd read the first time he'd gone through it.

The guy's license picture told him nothing. He was thirty-four, six-feet even, moderate weight, and completely unremarkable. He had light brown hair, with a shock of it swept across his forehead. He was attractive, but he wasn't particularly handsome. He looked like your average guy.

Goff darted back into the office. "Okay, Sam Price from PD was right around the corner from this feller's house. He knows the guy, too. Lives alone. Sam knows 'cause the guy filed a report of a trespasser that kept cutting through his yard at night. This was like six months ago. Turned out to be the sixteen-year-old girl lives behind him, sneaking back into her house."

"Okay."

"Anyway, he says there's no car in the driveway. Also, you can see the house plain as day from the lot where they park the buses at the school."

"Excellent," Evan said. "Have somebody get hold of the school and advise them we're going to be hanging out in their parking lot all day and night for the foreseeable future. Also, get one of our guys out in our parking lot right now, ready to tail."

"Done already," Goff said. "Meyers is out there already, pulled his own vehicle around from the back. Vi's checking the schedule to see who all we got to relieve him, and who can take which shift on the house."

"Thank you," Evan said. He puffed out a breath. "We need to know more about this guy. His records tell us nothing."

"See if he's got a Facebook," Goff said after a second.

Evan swung around to the desktop computer on the credenza behind him. He went to Facebook, pulled up thirteen Scott Wallers, and had just found the right one when Vi walked in.

"The surveillance details are being scheduled," she said.

"Thank you, Vi," Evan said without turning. "Okay, so this guy has a girlfriend, looks like. I mean, judging by every other picture on his Facebook page."

Goff looked over his shoulder. "Pretty thing."

Vi came to stand behind Evan. "Somebody should call her mother."

"Doesn't look like he posts too much," Evan said.

"Don't have too many friends, either," Goff said.

"Well, that doesn't mean anything," Evan said, a little defensively.

"Are you certain he still has this girlfriend?" Vi asked. "That last picture of them is from last year."

Evan checked, and she was right. He'd posted it from the previous summer. "How do we find out who she is?"

He heard Vi sigh behind him. "There's a tag. Her name is Elyse Leanne Price. If you click on her name, it'll pull up her page."

Evan clicked on it. "It's not doing anything."

Vi leaned over his shoulder. She smelled of cigarettes, Dentyne, and some kind of perfume.

"They're not friends," she said.

"What do you mean?"

"They're not Facebook friends. That's why it's not clickable." She adjusted her bifocals. "Click on his friends list."

Evan did, and they scrolled down the short list. She wasn't there.

"She might have deleted her Facebook account, gone on a social media break. Or they might have split," Vi said. "Put her name in the search bar up top, and let's see if we can locate her."

Evan did, and there was only one Elyse Price who was also Elyse Leanne. He clicked on it, and there she was, the same girl. Her profile picture was of her and a German Shephard on what looked like Cape San Blas beach.

"Scroll down," Vi said.

Evan did. The first post they saw was from Christmas Day, just under a month ago. It was from someone named Jimmy Price. The post was a picture of Elyse, which looked a few years old. She was standing in front of a Christmas tree with a smiling man in his fifties whose red hair matched hers. The post simply said, "Miss you, baby."

"Huh," Goff said.

Evan scrolled down a bit more, to find dozens of short posts from dozens of different people. They were from

November, most of them the first week of November, and all of them were some sort of memoriam or message of sympathy. Goff whistled.

"Oh, crap," Evan said quietly.

"Go further down," Vi said.

He did, all the way back to July. There weren't as many posts as he would expect from a young woman, and the last post she made herself was July 10.

"Where are the pictures of him?" Vi asked.

"What do you mean?" Evan asked her.

"All of those pictures he had of the two of them should be here somewhere as well," Vi said. "When you tag someone, it shows up on their page. Her photos are set to public, so they should be here."

"How do you know so much about Facebook?"

She frowned down at him like he was a simpleton. "Everybody over six knows about Facebook."

"I don't."

Vi sighed. "If I communicate with my relatives and ex-husband on Facebook, I don't have to actually spend any time with them in person."

"I thought your husband had passed away."

"Three of them did," she replied. "One is still living. Please wait to amuse yourself with black widow jokes until you get home. I've heard all of them already."

Evan made a point of not smiling as he stared at the screen. "Okay, so what about the pictures?"

"May I please drive?" she asked with a sigh. "It takes longer to give you instructions."

Evan stood up and let Vi take his seat. Goff grinned at him over Vi's head, but Evan pretended not to see it.

Vi clicked on the 'Photos' tab, and a new screen popped up with three different categories that Evan couldn't read from that distance. Vi clicked one, and a bunch of pictures came up. She scrolled through them at the speed of light.

"He's not here," she said with finality. "Not in the pictures he posted on his page, and not in any others, either."

"What are you saying? He Photoshopped pictures of his fake girlfriend?"

Vi turned around in his chair. "You're just being obtuse," she said sternly. "She deleted him. I suspect that at some point before she passed away, they broke up. Since he's still got pictures of her, I'd say she was the party who ended the relationship."

"Click back on his page, let's look at those pictures again," Evan said.

She did and clicked something to make all of the photos come up.

"Well, I was thinking maybe it was an imaginary relationship, or maybe just a friendship, but it does look like they were a couple," Evan said.

Vi clicked on a picture of the two of them at some kind of table. When it came up full-size, it turned out to be a picture taken in a restaurant, someplace expensive-looking. Waller was beaming and had an arm around the back of her chair, but she had a wan smile, and her hands were in her lap.

"Look," Vi said, pointing at the one comment on the photo, made by Waller. "Happy Valentine's Day, baby," Vi read. "She didn't reply."

Evan straightened up. "Okay. We need to know what the situation was between Waller and this woman, and we really need to find out how she died. Vi, can you track down this Jimmy Price and find out what the story was with the relationship? Then call the ME's office. If she was local, and she died of anything other than cancer or something, she might have been autopsied."

"Maybe he stabbed her, too, I'm thinking," Goff said as Vi left the room.

"Wouldn't that be convenient?" Evan asked, then felt like a horrible human being. He reached for his cigarettes. "You know what I mean. Come smoke with me."

"I don't smoke," Goff said, following Evan.

"Come chew gum."

Evan was on his third cigarette. Goff was still on his first piece of gum.

Evan felt like a coiled spring, ready for something to do besides give orders and wait. "Hey, did we check to see if Waller's DNA is in the database?"

"Nope, but the DNA we got isn't in the system, remember?"

"Right," Evan said thoughtfully, then took another drag. "Let's check anyway."

"If his DNA *is* in there, it means he's not our guy," Goff said. "Might kill your good mood."

"Kill my mood?" Evan asked. "I'd probably have to take some time off."

The back door scraped open and Vi came outside.

"Very well. I didn't reach Mr. Price, but I did reach his wife," she said as she joined them. "Her daughter *was* seeing Mr. Waller, for about three months, but she ended the relationship because she just wasn't as serious about it as he was. He wanted to settle down, and she wanted to travel. She was an English teacher, and she was thinking about teaching abroad."

She reached into one pocket of her short, caftan-like top, something with lavender flowers all over it. It matched her lavender capris, and the bright green Keds really pulled the outfit together, Evan thought. He watched her pull out one of those cases for cigarettes that he didn't know women still used. It was straw, with little palm trees on it, and "Barbados" embroidered on the front. She withdrew a Virginia Slim, and he leaned over and lit it for her.

"Thank you," she said, and blew out some smoke. "In any event, the family only met Mr. Waller twice, the mother said. Once at a barbecue early on in the relationship, and then at the funeral service."

"Did you ask how she died?" Evan asked her.

"I'm sorry. I was about to, but she became very upset and ended the call. I did, however, put in a call to young Mr. Coyle. He's in the middle of something, but he said he'd call you within the hour."

"Well, if it had been violent, you'd think she would have put two and two together with your calling her," Evan said. "What did you tell her you were doing?"

"Well, when we first started speaking, I simply said it was a background check," Vi answered. "But later, she asked me if there had been a problem with another woman. Of course, I told her it wasn't, but I find the question telling."

"It is," Evan agreed. "She didn't say anything about him being abusive or stalky or anything?"

"No, she did not, but I think she must have had some misgivings about the man, or her daughter shared things with her that she didn't choose to disclose to me."

"Okay." Evan lit another cigarette, which he really didn't want. He just needed the prop to help him focus.

He looked over at Goff, who was being unusually quiet. Goff was chewing slowly, staring at the back of their building.

"What's on your mind, Goff?"

"I lost one of Vi's husbands," Goff said without looking at him. "I can only count three."

Evan looked at Vi, who was frowning over at Goff. "You've really been married four times?" Evan asked her.

She turned her scowl on him. "I've now learned never to marry a poor Scrabble player, Mr. Caldwell. You simply can't ever respect them."

She ground her cigarette in the can of kitty litter they had for that purpose, then started back for the door. "I'll go see how that surveillance schedule is coming."

Evan took another drag. "I really want to go check this guy out. Just get a feel for him."

"I suppose you could go hang out at their urinals and hope he stops by," Goff said.

"I need a reason to go over there that wouldn't make him nervous." He ground out his cigarette. "I wish I hadn't already changed my license over."

"Want me to steal it?" Goff asked.

Evan gave him half a smile, then felt something fall into place in his head, with a very satisfying click.

TWENTY-TWO

EVAN WAS SIXTH in line, but it went surprisingly fast. He had no more than thirty minutes to watch Scott Waller as he waited, though there wasn't much to observe from across the room.

When it was his turn, he stepped up to the terminal of a young, blonde woman. Her nameplate said she was Emily Dermott. It didn't say she was the tallest woman working there, but he remembered.

When she asked how she could help him, he handed her his application for a replacement license and both halves of his current license.

"Oh, goodness, what happened here?" she asked him.

He tried to look sheepish without overdoing it. "I was cutting up my credit cards."

She smiled at him. "Oh, well, let's get you fixed up, Sheriff," she said.

He tried not to wince when she said it, but nobody was listening, and he figured it really wouldn't matter. He and other law enforcement officers were in the courthouse all the time. They were probably all easily recognizable.

She looked up from his application. "Oh, you forgot to check yes or no on whether you'd like to be an organ donor."

"Yes."

"I'll need you to check it, sorry."

She slid it over to him, and he checked the correct box. She spent a couple of minutes tapping away on her keyboard, then looked up at him. "Since this one's so recent, do you want to just keep the same picture?"

"No, I didn't love that one. I look sinister," he said, smiling.

"Oh, you look just fine," she said without flirtatiousness. After a moment, she made a final tap on her keyboard. "Okay, I've sent it down to the photographer. Go ahead and wait over there behind the green rope, and he'll be right with you."

"Thank you," Evan said.

He walked over to the other side of the room and waited behind two other people. He watched as Scott Waller took each picture. The man was polite without being friendly. He would look at his computer screen, call a name, and then instruct the person to stand against the wall. They would, and he clicked a little wand in his hand, told them thank you, and thirty seconds later he pulled their laminated license from the machine next to him. Then he told them to have a nice day and drive safely, and called the next person.

When it was Evan's turn, he waited to see if Waller was taken aback by the name. He wasn't, and he didn't seem to recognize Evan when he stood in the spot where he was told to, either. He was either a really good actor, or he didn't know who the Sheriff of Gulf County was.

He took Evan's picture, then waited for the machine. The license slid out, and he checked it for a few seconds, then held it out to Evan. "Here you go, sir. Thank you and drive safely."

"Thank you," Evan said, and walked away, license in hand.

His cell rang when he was halfway across the room. He answered it without looking at the number, holding it with his head as he pulled out his wallet.

"Caldwell."

"Oh, hey!" said Danny Coyle. "Sorry it took me so long to get back to you, right? But I was with Mitchell Overstreet's brother. Very disheartening."

"That's okay, Danny. Did you have a chance to look up that name?"

"Yeah, sure, sure. No autopsy done, per se, we just signed off on the hospital's COD," Danny said. "You know, for the death certificate. Required."

"Okay, so what was the cause of death?" Evan asked, trying without much luck to cram his new license into the little plastic window.

"Oh, acute liver failure. Yeah," he added somberly. "Not especially common to find severe liver toxicity due to chronic acetaminophen use. More common with intentional overdose. Suicide attempts, you follow?"

Evan glanced over his shoulder, but he was almost to the door, too far for Waller to overhear him. "Hold on one second, Danny," he said anyway.

"Oh, yeah, right, right. No problem."

Evan pushed open the door with his phone hand, then stopped by the front steps. He tucked the phone into his shoulder as he tried again to cram his license where it belonged.

"You're saying she died from acetaminophen?" he asked.

"Well, she died of liver failure, which was due to damage caused by acetaminophen use. Yeah. Her medical records confirmed she was a longtime user due to cluster headaches. Those are wicked as all get out, by the way." Danny took a breath. "Apparently, she didn't like going to the doctor, so by the time she started experiencing symptoms, she'd already been taking way more than the recommended daily dosage for some time."

"Okay," Evan said. "They can't treat that?"

"Well, early on, yeah, usually, but they didn't catch it early on," Danny answered. "She was only diagnosed four months before she died, right? Sadly, she passed away before they found a liver for her."

Evan stopped messing with his license. "Transplant you mean?"

"Oh, yeah. Don't get me started on the availability of healthy organs, right?"

Evan stared down at his license. There in red print, right beneath his signature, it stated that he was an organ donor.

"Crap, Danny, I gotta go," Evan said, and disconnected the call.

· ● ✳ ● ·

Evan was halfway down the hall to his office when Goff materialized from the bullpen and almost ran into him.

"Hey, boss, we got the surveil—"

"We have a motive," Evan interrupted as Goff fell into step with him. "I'm almost one hundred percent."

"What'd he do, confess?"

"No, come here and look."

They sped through Vi's area, but she was at lunch and unavailable to be offended. Evan swung around his desk and pulled the victim files front and center.

"The girlfriend, I forget her name—"

"Elyse."

"Yeah. She died of liver failure," Evan said as he started opening the files side by side.

DAWN LEE MCKENNA & AXEL BLACKWELL

"All right," Goff said.

"She died because she didn't get a liver transplant in time. Look." Evan tapped one photocopied license picture after another. "Not an organ donor. Not an organ donor. And not an organ donor." He looked at Goff.

"And they were all stabbed in the liver," Goff said, squinting.

"'You can't have it, either,'" Evan said.

"What?"

"The guy at the hotel," Evan said. "That's what he heard somebody yelling."

Goff raised his eyebrows. "I'll be dipped."

"We need to be on him like wet on water," Evan said, "and call your cousin. I want a list of every single person who got a license between October whatever— look up the date Elyse died—and today, who was *not* an organ donor."

"That could be a lot."

"Doesn't matter, we need to know who our potential next victims are," Evan said. "Go do that. I'm gonna request search warrants for his house, his car, his dog, whatever."

"You want to move on that now?" Goff asked, his eyebrows raised in disappointment.

"No, I don't want to spook him yet. I just want us to be ready. If we don't catch him stalking one of these people while he has the murder weapon in his pocket, we're gonna need something else to nail him."

"You scared me, there," Goff said quietly as he headed for the door.

"I'm a little hurt by that," Evan replied as he picked up his desk phone.

TWENTY-THREE

WALLER HAD ACHIEVED the lofty status of prime suspect, and as such, became the main recipient of the task force's resources. The mounting stacks of friends, associates, and business contacts from the three victims still needed to be cataloged and cross-referenced, on the off chance that Waller had the type of bad luck that would land him dead center in a murder spree he had nothing to do with creating, but no one expected that to be the case. Two sheriff's deputies and two officers from PSJ Police Department had been saddled with that chore.

Evan had moved Meyers and Crenshaw to the surveillance detail as a reward for their hard work and dedication on the initial wave of phone data. It was intended to be a reward, anyway. Meyers and Crenshaw might not have seen it that way, though. The county had two unmarked patrol vehicles, but anyone who knew any-

DAWN LEE MCKENNA & AXEL BLACKWELL

thing about vehicles would immediately recognize the silver Crown Vic or the dark blue Tahoe as undercover police, so Evan commandeered a small fleet of impounded vehicles to use for the surveillance operation. One Ford and two Chevy pick-ups, 90s era, and three wonderfully anonymous sedans in varying shades of beige. They all smelled funny, the most identifiable odors being pot, mildew and stale liquor. It was doubtful Scott Waller would notice one of them on his trail.

The fact that Waller worked directly across the street from the SO was a convenience appreciated by all the deputies. Evan received several requests that in the future, all suspects be chosen from a pool of people who worked in close proximity to the department. Evan said he'd see what he could do. But for all the joshing and banter, tension like a steel wire ran just below the surface. Evan had authorized overtime as needed to maintain two teams of deputies running continuous surveillance on Waller 24/7.

Vi had received, and passed on to Evan, the report from the DOL with the names of everyone who had been issued a license through the PSJ DOL since mid-October. Evan saw that Vi had highlighted nine of the names–those who had *not* checked the Organ Donor box. Three of those nine now rested in refrigerated stainless steel drawers, marred by more holes than they were born with. Evan intended to ensure that none of the other six joined them.

He didn't have enough manpower to maintain a watch on all six targets. It was also possible that Waller might go back through records to find non-organ donors from before his ex-girlfriend's death, in which case, his victim would not be on their list. Evan and Goff had debated warning the six potential targets; both had wanted to, but eventually decided against it. If denied his preferred victims, Waller wasn't likely to just give up and go home. He would probably find a different pool to attack, which would make the job of protecting them, and catching Waller, infinitely more difficult.

At the moment, Waller seemed to be comfortable, moving toward complacent. But if he became aware of Evan's interest in him, or his targets, that would change. If he had already begun stalking a new victim, and then that target radically altered their behavior, it might alert Waller that the authorities were closing in. If that happened, he would become much more dangerous.

In the end, Evan reluctantly opted to not notify the six but to maintain constant, double coverage on their suspect. He had also provided each deputy with the names, home addresses, and work addresses of the six targets, with orders to notify Evan if Waller came anywhere near them.

By Friday evening, two days into the roving stakeout, Waller hadn't given them anything. Evan sat in his rattan chair on the aft deck sipping his nightly golden milk, or what he called his turmeric tea.

The cold air carried the Dockside Grill's smoky aroma, mingled with the briny scent of the Gulf. Evan gazed out across the dark water. He was looking forward to the weekend, but only because it meant Quillen wouldn't be around.

The man had been demanding a quick resolution to the murders. Out of the other side of his mouth, he was fit to be tied about all the overtime money Evan had authorized. Evan offered to let Quillen fill in for one of the deputies, pro bono, which had ended the conversation quickly, but not well. If he had to choose one, Evan was glad it was the former. Evan expected the next conversation he had with Quillen wouldn't go much better unless the situation changed, quickly.

The buzz of his cell scattered his thoughts. "Caldwell," he answered.

"Hey, boss, it's Crenshaw," Jimmy said, sounding tense but excited. "I think we might have something."

"Tell me," Evan said.

"He's down here at Dixie Dandy. He was here last night, too, just parked beside the building, watching the store."

"Dixie Dandy," Evan asked. "What's a Dixie Dandy?"

"It's that gas station out FL-30. Highland Park, across from the beach," Crenshaw said as if he wondered how Evan could live in PSJ and not know that.

"That isn't on any of the target lists, is it?" Evan asked.

"It's not," Crenshaw said. "But it should be. Turns out Kate Randall *is* on the list, and she works here."

Evan sat up straight. "How'd we miss that?"

"It's her second job," Crenshaw said. "You've got her down as a secretary at the school, but she also works here three nights a week."

"You talked to her?" Evan asked, trying to keep the alarm out of his voice.

"Nah, Meyers did," Crenshaw said. "But don't worry, he was cool. Took his personal vehicle, drove right up to the front like a real person, got a soda and left. No way Waller could have known why he was there."

"Okay, good. Just keep it calm out there, real low-key," Evan said, even as he felt his own pulse quicken. He checked his watch as the hands crept toward eleven o'clock.

"You might want to roll some units this way, boss," Crenshaw said, "Store's about to close and where she's parked, she's going to have to walk right past his car."

Evan was on his feet. He went into the salon and grabbed his holster, wallet, and keys, and headed back out on deck.

"Look, do not let him get near her. Do your best to maintain cover, you blow it and we might never catch this guy, but first priority is Kate Randall's safety."

Evan hopped to the dock and started for the parking lot.

"Of course," Crenshaw said. Evan heard him passing instructions to Meyers. "She's locking up now, shutting off the lights… he's…crap!" Evan heard a thump, which he assumed was the cell hitting the seat. Or maybe the floor. In the background, Crenshaw urgently hissed at Meyers, "Go, go, go!"

Tires squealed. Evan listened as a confusion of muffled voices squawked over his cell. More squealing tires and honking horns. Evan hurried up the steps to the marina office and the parking lot beyond.

"Talk to me, Crenshaw!" Evan demanded. "Crenshaw! What's happening?"

The phone was now quiet. Evan jumped into his Pilot and jammed the keys into place.

Crenshaw finally responded, "False alarm. Sorry, boss."

This time it was Evan who was silent.

"You still there, Caldwell?" Crenshaw asked.

"What do you mean, 'false alarm?'" Evan forced himself to take a long slow breath.

"He didn't go for her," Crenshaw said. Evan could still hear the adrenaline in his voice, but it was on the ebb. "I mean, he *did* go for her, and we went to head him off, but another car pulled into the lot and Waller split."

"Did he make you?" Evan asked. He realized his right hand was aching. The steering wheel enduring its grip probably felt worse.

"No, no way," Crenshaw said, the smile evident in his voice. "We're in this old Ford that Beckett lent us from his impound. Meyers just played us off as a couple drunken idiots. He was pretty convincing."

"Yeah, I'm sure he was," Evan said with a sigh. "I heard you guys from here."

Crenshaw chuckled, but more from nerves than humor.

"What about Randall?" Evan asked. "Did she notice anything?"

"I doubt it," Crenshaw said. "Like I told you, another car pulled in just then. Ms. Randall was talking to the driver. Looked like she was giving them directions or something."

Evan took another long, slow breath. Let it out. Then did it again. Finally, he said, "Where is Waller now? Somebody still on him?"

"Oh, absolutely," Crenshaw assured. "Peters and Means are the second team out here. They were a bit farther back. Meyers has been updating them on the radio. He says they're still following Waller. Looks like he might just be going back to his house for the night."

Evan spent the next fifteen minutes grilling Crenshaw on every detail of the encounter, then instructed the deputy to file a report containing everything he had just related over the phone. Evan then repeated the routine with Meyers.

The report made him shudder just a bit; the fact that he had missed Randall's employment at Dixie Dandy bothered him. But, the certainty he now had about Waller counterbalanced his guilt. All he had to do was find a way to prove what he had just learned.

The almost icy breeze sucked his exhalations away in wispy puffs as he walked back across the parking lot to his boat. Proving it was always the hard part, but a plan was forming in Evan's mind, and he felt it was a good one.

TWENTY-FOUR

IT WAS SATURDAY NIGHT. They'd been in their positions since 9 pm, and every inch of skin covered by Evan's vest was itching. So was the ear in which his earpiece was sitting. It was ten to eleven, and Evan was going to shoot Scott Waller on sight because he itched.

Evan and Meyers were hunkered down behind an ice machine on the south side of the gas station, at the back. The front of the station faced FL-30 and the beach across the road. Goff was on his stomach over there in the sand and brush. On the north side of the building, Crenshaw, Peters, and Gordon were inside a low wall that enclosed a huge fuel tank.

That side of the station was on Pompano, and two empty cruisers were parked in the garage of a helpful resident four houses down. Evan's Pilot, which had brought him and Goff, was parked behind a defunct gas station on FL-30, two blocks south. An ambulance was waiting a few blocks away, parked with its lights off in an old boat storage shed.

The only car in the gas station lot was Kate Randall's little red Nissan pickup, parked in its usual spot.

Evan tried to rub his ear on his shoulder, which did nothing to alleviate his need to yank out the earpiece and rip his ear off his head.

He was checking his watch for the nineteenth time when Goff spoke quietly into his earpiece.

"Heads up. Suspect vehicle approaching from the south on thirty."

"Roger," PD Officer Jennifer Hansen answered from inside the station.

Evan pulled his service weapon from its holster, then keyed his shoulder mic. "Hold your positions until Goff has his location," he said quietly. He checked behind him. Meyers had his weapon at his side.

Goff's quiet voice came back over the radio. "Suspect's parked at the pump."

Evan keyed his mic. "Hansen, is she at the register?"
"Roger."

"He's out of the vehicle," Goff said. "Okay, he's seen her."
"Hansen, tell her to head back, then kill the lights."
"Roger."

Inside, Kate Randall, wearing a red uniform shirt and with her blonde hair in a ponytail, walked out from behind the register and headed for the back of the station, where the light switches were located, as was her routine.

"He's out of his vehicle," Goff said. "Behind the pump."

"Move into your positions," Evan said.

Evan hurried about ten yards toward the front of the station, stopping just shy of the corner of the building. As Meyers stopped behind Evan, the parking lot lights went dark.

· ● ✳ ● ·

Inside, Deputy Means was waiting with Kate Randall in the walk-in beer cooler. Hansen, wearing a red uniform shirt and with her blonde hair up in a ponytail, was making her way to the door. It wasn't a close match, but in the dark, and with nobody having any intention of letting Waller get within ten feet of Kate, it would do.

"Hansen's coming out," Goff said.

"On Goff's go," Evan said.

He listened as the bell over the door jangled, then he could hear Hansen shake the locked door as though to check it. He heard keys jangling.

"Knife," Goff said quietly.

Evan blinked salty sweat from his left eye, raised his gun in a two-handed grip. He was expecting to hear the door to the Nissan open when Goff spoke again.

"Go!"

Evan charged around the corner, Meyers behind him and moving ahead and to Evan's left. "Gulf County Sheriffs! Drop your weapon!"

Crenshaw and the other deputies were coming around the north side, all yelling commands for Waller to freeze, drop to his knees, and drop his weapon.

Evan was on the passenger side of the pickup. Hansen was about a foot from the driver's door, spinning and pulling her weapon. Behind her, about five feet away, stood Scott Waller, momentarily frozen, his eyes and mouth wide. In his right hand, something narrow glinted in the light from the streetlamp.

"Get down!" Evan yelled, walking, knees slightly bent, arms stiff and out front, toward the back of the pickup. "Drop your weapon, now!"

Waller's right knee bent just a bit. He crouched slowly, lowering the knife almost to the gravel. Then he burst forward, raised blade gleaming in the ambient light. He had taken one running step toward the woman he still might have believed was Kate Randall, when his right knee exploded like a water balloon filled with chili. Half a second later, Evan heard the report from Goff's rifle.

He and the deputies had closed the distance to Waller almost before his face hit the ground. The knife skittered out of his hand, and Hansen kicked it away as Evan reached the man. Waller rolled over on to his back, his face twisted in pain, but without making a sound.

Evan and the other deputies kept their weapons trained on Waller until Crenshaw had jerked him onto his stomach, and zip-tied his wrists. Only then did Waller start screaming.

Evan looked up as he heard boots in the gravel on his left. Goff stopped beside him, rifle down, and twitched his mustache as he looked down at Waller.

"Nice," Evan said.

"I figure little Tina would probably think so," Goff said, almost under his breath.

TWENTY-FIVE

SUNDAY MORNING WAS the warmest they'd had in weeks. It was supposed to be in the sixties by noon, and on his way to Sunset Bay, Evan had been pleased to hear the radio say there'd be a bit of wind and a nice, light chop.

Evan had decided that, for his physical health and mental function, he needed to stop hiding in his work, and spend more time actually living his life. Now that Scott Waller had been arrested, he really didn't have an excuse for overwork.

A search of Scott Waller's home had produced a good deal of information. His laptop showed hundreds of pictures of him and Elyse during their relationship, and several emails he'd sent and received. The most significant emails were the ones going back months, emails to Elyse that Gmail had returned as undeliverable.

Also on the laptop were hundreds of emails to organizations that supported or facilitated organ transplants, to people found through news stories who had gotten transplants, and to surgeons who specialized in organ transplantation. It looked like Waller had believed that if he found her a healthy liver, she might take him back. If she hadn't passed away, Evan and Goff had wondered aloud if Waller would have been crazy enough to actually kill someone for it.

On the other hand, it might have been her death that moved him from the category of mentally unbalanced to violently mad. The background they'd gotten so far from family members and physicians indicated that Waller had been troubled since his teens, and in therapy. He had also had two other relationships that had ended because he was too clingy, too serious, too invested.

Whatever Waller's mental state might be, Evan was pretty sure they'd be able to prove he was sound enough to be held responsible for his crimes. The media was certainly excited about the arrest, and consequently so was James Quillen. Evan was pretty sure they'd drag the story out until they could begin exhaustive reports on the trial.

Until there was a trial to deal with, Evan was eager to put Waller out of his mind and to get his mind off his work, even if just for a couple of days. However, once he was sitting by Hannah's bed, he fell right into the habit of talking to her about work. It was something he had almost exclusively avoided before her accident, but now, ironically, it had become habit.

He sat in the mauve upholstered chair, next to the picture of him and Hannah on their cruise. It had been taken the day they'd stopped at Coco Cay. Evan remembered the water, as clear as bottled and such an unrealistic shade of blue that it looked like Disney had created it. It had been the first time he'd ever managed to float, and Hannah had teased him about that, with all of his surfing and his love for the sea.

On a side table near the window, a vase held a large bouquet of lilies, Hannah's favorite flower. They'd been a regular gift to her during their marriage, and if she was hurt that he wasn't more creative, she hadn't let him see it.

Evan had opened Hannah's blinds, and the sun streaked across her bed in narrow lines the color of store-brand butter. When he'd arrived an hour earlier, and bent to kiss her forehead, her skin had been slightly tacky and smelled of gardenia. Someone had been using the lotion he'd brought a few weeks back, and he was grateful for it. Hannah had used it by the gallon since he'd known her.

"Anyway," Evan said, as he leaned forward to stretch his back. "Tina Vicaro's service is tomorrow. Bellamy's family took him back to Tallahassee so he could be buried with his parents. I'm not sure what Overstreet's family is planning."

He stood up, arched his back, then straightened and put a hand on her bed rail. "By the way, I've changed your cat's diet, and it appears to have been a worthwhile effort. I've been finding much fewer furry black cocktail franks around the boat. I don't know how a cat can throw up so much and still be so huge."

Hannah's monitors beeped and clicked beside him, marking the time for him, in case he forgot how long he'd been having one-sided conversations with his wife.

"I'm also conducting some experiments on the little jerk," Evan went on. "I have a project, which I can't disclose to you at this time, but to that end, I tried getting him to wear a halter. Unfortunately, he just laid there like a roped calf, but I tried something new last night and I think I might be onto something. I'll let you know how it works out."

He stared down at Hannah, at the square line of her jaw, which he'd always thought so elegant, the curve of the chin that she'd complained was too pointy.

"I should go," he said after a few minutes. "I'll see you tomorrow."

He leaned over the rail and kissed her cheek.

"I hope you like the lilies."

· ● ✳ ● ·

From the helm, Evan smiled over at Sarah, who was standing on the dock on his port side, waiting for his word to free the Sea Fox's stern line. She shook her head at him and raised her voice to be heard over the outboards.

"He's not gonna go for it, dude. It's just not…natural for him to be like that."

Evan smiled at her. "I'm telling you, we practiced it for two hours last night. It's cool."

"Yeah, I see all the scratches up and down your arms, man."

Evan grabbed the kill switch and clipped it to his belt loop. "Look, either come with us or don't. Either way, shut up and get the stern line."

She licked at her bottom lip. "I'm coming with you, dude. If he freaks out, somebody's gotta grab him." She frowned at him, her finely designed black eyebrows edging toward her little nose. "His tail. Make sure he's not on his tail. It'll hurt his little…tailbones or whatever."

"He knows how to operate his own tail, Sarah."

He shook his head at her, then turned back around as he heard her hit the deck with a light thump. He eased the bow further to starboard, then pulled out and around the Chris-Craft.

Sarah came to stand on his left, her hand on the back of the captain's seat he almost never used. He preferred to stand, to feel the vibration travel upward from the soles of his feet. It was the closest thing to surfing that he could manage without a board.

As they made their way out of the no-wake zone, he could feel her eyes on him. He glanced over at her. She was staring at his chest.

"Chill out, kid."

The night before, he'd dug out an old canvas knapsack that he'd hung onto since college. After the first few attempts to stuff Plutes into it, he'd understood how dramatic a statement 'letting the cat out of the bag' really was. On the fifth or sixth try, Plutes had gone in under protest, but not before ripping him to shreds trying to get out. Putting him into the knapsack while Evan was wearing it backwards, on his chest, was a little more of a production.

"I'm like seriously concerned that you've just found some new way to torture this cat because he pees in your shoes."

"Relax."

They passed out of the marina and into the bay, and Evan opened it up just a little. He felt a shuffling against his stomach and looked down. The flap of his knapsack was twitching. Evan looked back up to make sure the way was still clear, though the closest other boat was fifty yards to port and on the hook.

He eased around the northern end of the peninsula and gave the boat a bit more throttle.

"Don't go too fast," Sarah yelled into the wind.

"Stop whining," he yelled back.

His pack shifted again, and he glanced down. Plutes had stuck his head out from under the flap and was squinting into the wind. His ears were flattened, and his whiskers were pinned back to his cheeks. His fur rippled and danced like black water.

Evan grinned. He might not be a cat lady, but he was pretty sure he could find his way around this particular cat. Plutes shifted around in the canvas bag, then stretched his neck like he was doing his best cormorant impression.

"He's freaking out!" Sarah yelled.

Evan looked back down and smiled, and he realized it was the first time in a long time that he'd smiled so hard it almost hurt his cheeks.

Evan cut the wheel a bit and started steering in an easy, graceful slalom.

"No, he's not," Evan said. "He's surfing."

THANK YOU FOR READING
DEAD CENTER

WE HOPE YOU had fun with the second book in the Still Waters Suspense series. If you missed the first book, *Dead Reckoning*, you can find it here:

AMAZON.COM/DP/B075FL22C9

To get a heads-up for each new release, and to find out about discounts, free books, and public appearances, you can sign up for the mailing list here:

DAWNLEEMCKENNA.COM

You might also enjoy Dawn Lee McKenna's original series, the Forgotten Coast Florida Suspense series, which is set in Apalachicola, FL, and which introduces the character of Evan Caldwell. You can find that series, as well as Dawn Lee's Southern fiction novel, See You, here:

AMAZON.COM/GP/PRODUCT/B079DTTWH2

All are available on Kindle Unlimited.

If you are interested in something a little out of the mainstream, have a look at Axel Blackwell's paranormal thrillers here.

AMAZON.COM/AXEL-BLACKWELL/E/B00W0I2UO4

You can also visit the Dawn Lee McKenna Facebook page, where you'll find pictures of locations and people used in both series, updates on new books, news about author events, and a lot of odd people, including Dawn Lee.

FB.COM/DAWN-LEE-
MCKENNA-1470505269903994/

ABOUT THE
AUTHORS

DAWN LEE MCKENNA is the author of the novel
See You, and the bestselling *Forgotten Coast Florida Suspense*
series. A native of Florida, she now lives in northeastern
Tennessee with her five children and one domineering cat.

AXEL BLACKWELL grew up in one of those small
Indiana towns where the only fun is the kind you make
yourself. Many ghost and UFO sightings in central
Indiana between 1985 and 1990 can be attributed to
Axel and his brothers attempting to escape boredom.
Axel now lives with his family and an assortment of
animals in the Pacific Northwest.